DEADLY
DECEPTION
-PRELUDE-

P.J. MANN

ACKNOWLEDGEMENT

A special thanks goes to my editor Tricia Drammeh, who went through the whole document to make it shine, and it's indeed shining. My followers, friends, and subscribers for their continuous encouragement.

CHAPTER 1

I'm a liar... a filthy liar.

The problem is I don't even realize whether I'm telling a lie or not. Apparently, my brain records the facts, but it distorts them when I need to recall them. Because of my behavior, I've lost friends, family, and relationships. Then, one day, an article came to my attention. It was about pathological liars, and the more I read it, the more I found similarities in the story of my life. For this reason, at the age of twenty-three, I decided to seek psychiatric help.

So, there I was, sitting in the waiting room of a psychiatrist, waiting for the door to open and someone to call my name. If you are familiar with the waiting rooms of healthcare institutions, you might have experienced how difficult it is sometimes to mind your own business, avoiding staring at the other patients. On that occasion, despite my efforts, I failed in my purpose.

The annoyed stare of the man seated in front of me literally stabbed me. With an audible growl, he grabbed a newspaper and started to read, making sure to cover his face. Unwillingly, that man gave me what appeared to be a brilliant idea. Therefore, I chose a magazine too and browsed for something interesting, in the hope of keeping myself busy and diverting my focus from the unnerving wait.

Nothing in particular was able to catch my attention, only a couple of articles on international politics and travel advertisements. Those weren't enough to kill some time. Disappointment overwhelmed me when, glancing at the clock, I realized not only did I not kill time, but it wasn't even wounded. Placing the magazine back on the table, I took a visual tour of the environment, noticing every detail in the room.

Surprisingly, it came to my mind how the waiting rooms of healthcare institutions resemble each other. They all have an "ill," neutral look, and in my opinion, if a person isn't sick, after having spent a few hours inside, they'll start feeling unwell. Perhaps it's a way to increase the number of illnesses to be treated. While I was deep into my own considerations, I must have lost track of time because, against all the odds, the doctor himself appeared at the door, calling me. Like a spring, I jumped from my chair and walked toward the door. I took a fast glance around, hoping to find a healthier environment. With my greatest disappointment, the same gray walls and monotonous floor pattern were also repeated in his office. The only thing breaking that colorless world was the dark brown desk, matched by the color of the couch.

"So, Mr. Jackson, would you like to tell me how I can help you?" The doctor kept a calm tone, smiling kindly at me.

Inhaling deeply, I tried to find the right words. "I'm not sure how am I going to explain my problem, but I'm a liar." Taking a short pause allowed me to observe his reaction to my statement. "You see, I do my best to recall details and events as closely as possible to reality. However, what comes out of my mouth turns out to be a lie, and I don't understand how this can happen. Once I read about people who have this same problem. If I remember right, it's called compulsive lying."

"I see," he muttered, glancing at me through narrowed eyelids. "This is fascinating. Indeed, we can document a few cases of people who can't stop telling lies. Some people try to gather attention, admiration, or sympathy. There have been some attempts to outline the differences between a pathological and a nonpathological lie, but more research is necessary to make appropriate distinctions.

"A key feature of a pathological lie is that it has no obvious motivation. In your case, you don't have the slightest idea you're telling a lie. But while your illness is interesting, not only is it a bit more rare

3

than the non-pathological case, but also harder to treat. With this, I mean that I need to understand about you and your way of lying."

"Of course." I still hoped he could find a way to help me out.

"Can you give me some example of your problem? Can you recall any particular event when your parents or your friends caught you in one of your lies?"

In any other occasion, I could list thousands of examples about my habit, but you know how it goes– as soon as you must recall something, your mind becomes a blank screen. Closing my eyes, I tried to focus on something, anything.

"Yes!" I exclaimed, as out of the blue, one case came to mind. "This happened last week. Stewart is a friend of mine, who's a football fanatic. We decided to go to the Sunday game, and he asked me to buy the tickets for both of us."

Taking a short pause, I recalled the events. "Now, on Friday afternoon, he asked me if I had the tickets, and I replied that I had them in my backpack. Recalling clearly that I went to the booth, made the purchase, and exchanged some chit-chat with the seller, I was certain I'd bought them.

"He came to my place to get his ticket and to pay me, but I couldn't find them. We searched the whole place without any success, then he asked me if I was sure I bought them. Of course, I was. I also remembered having paid with my credit card.

"At that point, Stewart asked me to check my bank account because he started to doubt I purchased them. Do you believe it? The payment didn't show, meaning one thing: I didn't buy the tickets."

I shook my head in disappointment, thinking about how stupid I must have appeared to him, but to be honest, I still remember I got them.

The doctor glanced at me with a stern expression. "Have you experienced any other physical discomforts, like increasing headaches, vertigo, nausea, sudden change of mood?"

Trying my best to recall the last time I even had a headache, let alone the other symptoms he listed, I shook my head. "No, I don't remember any of those episodes."

"That's reassuring, as we might exclude tumors, at least in this first stage. Moreover, pathological lying disorder has been associated mostly with factitious or personality disorders. Indeed, it's an interesting case. I intend not only to understand more about this illness but also to find a treatment."

His understanding and empathy reached my soul, and the certainty of being close to the solution to my problems slowly took root in my restless mind. Nevertheless, I was concerned when he mentioned the word "illness." Did he mean I was going insane?

"I'm afraid to ask, but will I be locked up in an asylum for the rest of my life?"

He smiled broadly at me. "Not all illnesses require treatment in a hospital. You might have misunderstood your problem."

"Since you mentioned mental illness, I worry about either being locked up or being prescribed with strong drugs. So, what's the plan? A psychiatric facility, or being turned into a drugged-out zombie?" A slightly sarcastic note in the tone of my voice accompanied my question.

He considered me for a second, then laughed heartily. "I can see you are a man of humor, and I like it. Don't you worry; nothing like this will be necessary."

"Will I have to go through a series of psychotherapy sessions, or something similar?" The unpredictability of where this discussion was leading intrigued me.

His brows knitted together, creasing his forehead. "As I told you before, your case isn't easy to treat, and I can't offer any absolute cure. The illness itself is relatively rare; therefore, it isn't fully understood in its complexity. I'm afraid to tell you there's very little I can do to help you."

"You mean I came here for no reason?" My hopes crashed down.

"This isn't entirely correct. I said there aren't therapies that can, for sure, cure you." He took a short pause. "I'll try to be clearer. I've been working with a colleague of mine at the University on similar cases. All the conventional treatments were destined to fail miserably, but we developed a non-conventional one, which, in theory, should help people like you. Our project met the interest of the scientific community and some private institutions. Thanks to them, we have access to substantial funding for our research. What we're missing is a patient. If you agree, you can be part of it, and with some luck, your condition might improve."

It was like God Himself came down from the Heavens to give me a blessing, and my hopes came back in force. However, I started to think about what their treatment was about.

What kind of risks are involved?

"Will it be dangerous? Are you going to electroshock me?" I was exploring all the possibilities swirling in my mind.

"I'm proposing six months of travel, wherever you desire." A half-smirk appeared on his face as he tilted his head to one side.

"T-travel? I don't have any money to leave for half a year, and I have my job. I can't leave for such a long period," I objected.

"As I told you, we'll use the funds for the research." He leaned back in his chair. "The only things you will have to pay for will be your personal expenses, like food and drinks. Concerning your work, we'll explain to your employer your need to take medical leave. You will always wear a camera, which will be remotely connected with our laboratory at the University. It will record every single move you make. Therefore, I'm afraid you won't have any privacy during this period.

"You can't check the content of the camera. This is because you will have to submit to us a sort of daily journal about everything you can recall about the day you had," the doctor continued. "Every week, we'll send the corrected version of your daily report to you, and we'll underline what and how it went wrong. You should use some time to focus on the corrections we underlined and compare it with your memories."

"Hold on. Are you telling me that you will pay me to take a six-month vacation and to write a diary every day?" I was almost sure I understood it right, but those kinds of proposals happen only in the movies.

"This is exactly what I mean. Every Sunday, we'll send you some tests, which you will submit at the end of the day." He crossed his hands on his lap as he explained how things would work out.

"I don't know what to say," I hesitated doubtfully. "On the one hand, I don't think I have anything to lose by accepting your proposal. After all, if it works, then I'm ready to take the chance and go for a long vacation. Jesus. Last time I went on vacation, I was ten years old." The toes of my feet curled with excitement.

The doctor looked at me with a broad smile. "Fantastic. I'll write a letter to your supervisor, so you won't have anything to worry about. Now, coming back to factitious or personality disorders. I would like to have a chat with you and do some further tests to assess your situation better. I will ask you questions aimed to go deeper into your problem. They might sound at times too personal, but I want you to answer them as honestly as possible. I'm not going to judge your personal life; I need to know everything that is going on in your mind." He invited me to get more comfortable on the couch.

***

After forty-five minutes worth of quite personal and uncomfortable questions, I was extremely glad to return to sit on the chair in front of his desk, and he wrote a letter for my supervisor.

"Here you are, Mr. Jackson. This is for your employer." He gave me the envelope. "It explains the need for you to take an extended medical leave. It's foreseeable that he won't be enthusiastic, but on the other hand, you have the right to be treated."

A light shake, like an electric shock, ran through my skin as my hands touched the letter. That was tangible proof that I didn't imagine anything; it was real, and I was excited.

Walking the streets, I couldn't believe what had happened. I pondered whether my mind was still distorting reality, or I was involved in a project that would send me on vacation for six months.

Still, trying to make some sense of the last three hours, I reached home. As soon as I came in, Moses, my cat, came to greet me. His presence brought me back to the place where I was.

He never judged me for being a liar. Whether he understood it or not, he had always been there, when I was crying or when I was laughing.

I owe him more than he can ever imagine. "Hello, Buddy. Did you miss me?"

"Meow," he purred contently as I scratched his head.

Like a shot, I realized I couldn't bring him with me, and it would be terrible for him to live in kennel, a sort of prison for pets. *Half a year is a long time,* I pondered.

With a sigh, I turned my head to him. "I'm wondering how to make you understand my absence."

I went to the kitchen to eat a small snack, when the phone started to ring. "Hello." I kept checking in the fridge for something to satisfy my hunger.

"Ethan, my old buddy, how are you?" Stewart's cheerful voice came to my ears.

Stewart was one of the few friends who remained at my side. We'd known each other since high school, and he was the only one able to stand my lies, trying patiently to correct them whenever he'd acknowledge them. People don't want to have anything to do with guys like me, as I'm considered nothing but trouble.

"Oh, hi. I went to the doctor to figure out a solution to my problem." It wasn't easy, not even in front of my best friend, to talk about my lying habit.

"My dear Ethan, for that issue, I think a simple injection of honesty would be sufficient," he sneered sarcastically.

"Well, for your information, I don't lie because I want to do so. This is a real illness, and for how rare it is, it doesn't have many options to be cured, at least with conventional medicine," I snapped, regretting having mentioned my visit to the psychiatrist.

He just couldn't understand how it feels being aware of something wrong in your brain. Being mocked is something I consider rude and inappropriate.

"Okay. Sorry, Ethan. I didn't mean to be offensive. So, what did the doctor say, besides confirming that you are a pathological liar?" He tried to move on from an embarrassing moment.

11

"Dr. Wright suggested I be part of some sort of research he's undertaking with one of his colleagues at the University," I told him.

Once again, I opened the letter the doctor wrote to my supervisor to be sure I wasn't going to tell another lie. "I'll have to undertake a half-year trip to different locations and keep a diary of everything I've seen during each day, trying to recall everything with the maximum accuracy."

I sat down on the couch, still keeping my eyes on the letter. "Meanwhile, a camera will always be connected to tell them what happened. They'll send me their corrected version of my diary, and I'll have to take some time to analyze and to remember." My hand slowly caressed the smooth fabric.

Believe me, that sounded like a lie to myself, even if it wasn't.

A long pause of silence fell between us, making me wonder whether he'd ended the conversation, tired of my fabrications. Then, I heard him burst out in laughter. "You have been telling lies all your life, but this is the most absurd of all. How do you expect me to believe something like this?" he laughed, amused. "It reminds me of that time you told me you received a reply about your dream job. You were so excited about their feedback and how impressed they were with your resume. Then, when I read it, it was another automated answer by which you weren't selected for the interview. Or the time when you had that girlfriend of yours-"

"Yeah, yeah." All the positive feelings I gathered during the day seemed to disappear with Stewart's mocking. "I remember those cases, but this time is different, and I don't know what to say. Believe me when I say, I've read to you what the doctor wrote to me and to my supervisor at work to justify my absence. It sounds crazy, and if I weren't reading this paper to you, I'd have thought I was lying, too." I observed what Moses was doing.

"Really?" His voice turned grave. "May I also have a look at it, so I can confirm you are not inventing everything again?"

"Yes. I can show you the letter. I'm not kidding, and this isn't a lie, for once. By the way, I'll need someone to look after Moses."

"Would you prefer that I bring him to live with me, or for me to come to your place every day to give him food and play with him?" he suggested.

"Well, you decide. I'd prefer you to take Moses with you. That way, he'll have all the attention and the company he might need. And if he needs the vet, you'd be able to care of his health." I began to consider the advantages of having my cat moved to Stewart's house.

"Sure. He can stay here with me. At least Molly will have someone to play with. By the way, Moses is fixed, isn't he? She hasn't yet been sterilized, and

I wouldn't like to have to separate them from your cat's harassment."

"Don't you worry. He's been neutered, and he has always been a gentle cat. You make sure it isn't Molly who assaults Moses." The tone of our conversation returned to a more normal one.

"She's only a kitten. She isn't jumping over every male she finds."

"Well, anyway, Moses is neutered, so he won't be a threat to Molly's virginity. You can be sure of that. Should I presume you are going to keep him at your home?" I wanted to be sure that he meant to take charge of Moses' care during my absence.

"Sure. Why not? No problem. Get well and be back safe, sound, healed, and tanned, you lucky one," he said with a slight tone of envy in his voice.

"I'll try to do my best. By the way, did you call me only to ask about the result of my first day of therapy, or did you have something else to say?"

"I assumed that since today is Friday, we might have some fun downtown. What do you say?"

With everything that happened, I almost forgot about what day it was, and his reminder left me speechless for a moment.

"Sure. What time?"

"Hmm, let's see. I can come to pick you up in a couple of hours. Will it be too early for you?"

"It will be perfect. See you soon. Bye." Ending the conversation, I started to prepare for the evening; I needed to eat something first.

As I ate, I took out a world map, trying to figure out where I'd like to travel. Since the trip would be mostly paid, I decided to start with all the destinations I'd never been able to afford, but would love to visit.

"Wow. The world is huge; so many countries I don't have the slightest idea about," I pondered.

Africa was one of the continents which interested me the most. Besides the natural wonders, I thought about the history of each country. Recalling the colonialist period, the revolts, the internal conflicts between ethnic groups and tribal heritage, my mind was captured, and I needed to visit those places, as the chance arrived.

So many countries, and so many adventures were opening in front of me. Yet, with the excitement, there was a growing discomforting feeling of uncertainty. Something I could only sense, which resembled mostly a warning.

CHAPTER 2

That same evening, in Dr. Wright's studio

As the last patient of the day left the room, Dr. Wright returned to look at the preliminary data he gathered about Ethan. He was sure he would be an exact match for the test and couldn't wait another day before talking to Prof. Doyle. Regardless of the late hour, he grabbed his phone, with his eyes steady on the notes he'd been writing down, and dialed Prof. Doyle's number.

"Doyle," he replied as he was driving home.

"Jason, this is Bernard. Do you have a minute to talk?"

Keeping his eyes on the road, Prof. Doyle said, "Sure, I'm in my car, so for the next thirty minutes, I'm all ears."

"Well, today I had a new patient, which I believe to be the perfect candidate for the test. I know I could wait to tell you about him tomorrow, but I wouldn't be able to sleep," he chuckled.

"Interesting. What kind of pathology does he have?" Prof. Doyle wondered.

"He's a pathological liar, and according to the first impression I had about him, he is exactly the kind of person we're looking for. Shy, mild-natured..." He kept glancing at his notes.

Prof. Doyle remained silent for a moment, pondering about the potential patient his colleague was proposing. "He sounds a very interesting case, indeed. We'll need to test him more thoroughly and submit our results to our client. You know the drug we're testing requires, at this stage, an exact fit in personality. He isn't willing to spend money on useless trials. Also we should keep in mind that our test requires victims."

A grin appeared on Dr. Wright's face. "I know that, and I've already sent a message to our client for approval. I was also thinking that, for this time, we might move everything abroad." He took a short pause to collect his thoughts. "A murder in this same city or State might raise too much attention, and considering the generosity of the funds we are allowed, it would be safer to switch the operations somewhere else. At least this is something we can try."

Not sure he understood correctly, Prof. Doyle pulled to the side of the road to focus better on what his colleague was saying.

"Hold on a minute, are you saying that..."

"Exactly that," Dr. Wright interrupted. "I have offered my patient to travel for six months. If our client accepts our suggestion, we will avoid the risk of being accused of murder."

"And in this case, the one who will face the consequences will be our patient...That's both brilliant and wicked," The voice of Prof. Doyle flickered. "Let me know what our client replies."

The sound of an incoming message on his computer informed Dr. Wright about a prompt reply from their client. Almost fearing his reaction, he opened it, holding his breath, as his heartbeat started increasing its pace.

It took a few moments to read the short message received, to make sure he'd understood it.

Then with a long exhale, he collapsed, leaning on his chair. "I just received his reply. He agrees to our proposal. He didn't define it as wicked, but he called it brilliant too."

"Then you have only one thing left: send me all the documentation you have about him and I will contact him for the other necessary tests we'll need to perform," Prof Doyle replied, relieved. He started up the engine, to resume his journey home.

"Sure, I'm doing it right away. Have a nice evening!"

As soon as he ended the conversation with his colleague, Dr. Wright hurried to forward him all the details, notes and information he'd taken that day.

Moving the operation abroad might be the best way to keep our testing out of sight of the Police. They must be kept as far as possible from this project. He clenched his fists and stood from his chair, ready to go home and stop thinking about that project.

CHAPTER 3

Saturday, from the moment I woke up until the late afternoon, I pondered all the things that happened lately: the meeting with Dr. Wright and his crazy proposal, traveling to cure my lying behavior, the afternoon and evening with Stewart, and all the fantasies about visiting as many places in the world as I could imagine.

Once again, I took the letter in my hands, and I read it another couple of times. However, the more I did so, the more I found it impossible that something so amazing could happen to me. I've no idea how many times I went through it. I was afraid my brain had messed up the events, and what I remembered was a lie. For the whole afternoon, my mind was focused on my journey, the meeting, and all the details I was desperately trying to remember correctly.

A slight discomfort, mixed with a reasonable amount of paranoia about the possibility of falling into a well-set trap, possessed me as I was alone with my thoughts. Loneliness was not the best ally, and grabbing my telephone, I called the only person in this world who could rescue me from myself: Stewart. He said he would come to my place as soon as possible. Therefore, I had to rely on the second presence which would give me any sort of relief from the storm slowly brewing in my mind, and that was Moses.

The doorbell ringing interrupted my considerations.

"Meow?" Moses glanced at me with his bright green eyes.

"I guess this is Stewart. Don't be jealous." I walked to open the door, followed by Moses.

"Ethan! How are you doing?" He came in, giving me a fist bump.

"Can't complain. How about you?" I closed the door behind him.

Raising a bag to the height of his shoulders, he walked into the living room. "Since it's getting late, I thought we might have dinner together. I picked up something from the Chinese restaurant. I hope that's okay with you."

"That's more than okay!"

We both sat down at the table, followed by a curious Moses, who came to join us. Stewart had traveled a lot in the past, and he knew many things about the places that were worth visiting, and others to be avoided. We scanned the map. Every single country has many interesting things to be seen, but I needed to focus on just a few of them. It took the whole evening to set up a draft of the plan. It was late in the night when, tired and satisfied, we examined the final version of the details for my world tour. The first leg of the journey would travel through Africa. In the first month, I'd visit Morocco, Ghana, Togo, and Benin. The last two countries would be easy to cross, considering they are more extended in a North-South direction than in an East-West orientation. Then I'd move to Nigeria, and from there, I might fly to South Africa and travel North through Zambia and Zimbabwe. This would take another four or five weeks, depending on the schedule to follow. At this point, my second leg of the journey would start, and that would be in Asia.

This was, perhaps, the part which would take more time to travel along, because of the vastness of the whole continent and the countries I wanted to visit. Therefore, from Zimbabwe, my journey would continue to Georgia and Azerbaijan, then India and Nepal, China, and Russia. From there, it was almost a natural transition to reach Europe and visit Finland, Norway, and Sweden, moving to Germany, France, Switzerland, Austria, Italy, and Spain. I was interested in visiting all the European countries, but my trip wasn't long enough to allow me to do so. After that, I'd be back in Boston, in the hope the therapy yielded the hoped-for results.

"Well, now, it looks like you will have a fabulous vacation." Stewart's voice betrayed a slight shade of envy.

"So it seems, but I still have some doubts about it."

"What do you mean? Do you think we should add something more?"

"No. I'm afraid they won't accept my proposal. Maybe I'm shooting too high, or I'm too greedy," I started to consider. "What if they think I'm abusing the offer, and they'll search for someone else...someone who doesn't ask for such an expensive plan?"

Stewart placed a hand on my shoulder. "Listen, you have no reason to be paranoid. You are not easily replaceable, because your illness isn't so common. Think about it for a moment. If they consider your suggestion outside of the budget, they'll ask you to modify it. I don't think they'll search for someone else."

He was probably right, but I wasn't reassured in any way. A tiny nagging voice inside me told me to forget about this plan. *How can a trip change what you are? If it were this easy, then they would have developed this sort of therapy earlier*, I thought. That voice seemed to warn me of something I couldn't even fathom. Nevertheless, it was also true that I hadn't the slightest idea about what they intended. I wasn't a psychiatrist, so I had no means to judge their methods. For this reason, I followed the advice of the other voice in my head and stopped thinking about it.

Stewart glanced the clock. "Now, it's time for me to leave. Will you be able to stand the loneliness?" he joked with a melodramatic tone of voice. "Moses, take care of your friend here because I'm afraid I don't trust him at all. Luckily, in this house, someone has some sense left."

"I think I can manage to be on my own. Thank you for everything. I'll keep you informed of their answer." I pushed him to the door.

"You'd better do so, or I won't talk to you anymore, and I won't take Moses with me during your absence."

Monday morning, I arrived at work earlier than usual, and I decided to put the letter my psychiatrist wrote to my supervisor on his desk. Courage has never been one of my strong points, and I couldn't find the guts to go and talk to him, explaining what was going on. Shame at the idea of admitting my lying problem rose from the depth of my soul. He didn't need to have details about my illness, but on the other hand, part of me wanted him to be aware and perhaps sympathize with my problem. I wasn't sure how to react if he asked me the nature of my illness or why I needed such an extended period of leave.

After a couple of hours of steady work, my supervisor arrived in my office. Without knocking, gingerly peeking inside the door, his creased forehead told me everything about the reason for his visit.

"Hello, Ethan, I need to talk to you," he started, with evident embarrassment in his voice. Closing the door behind him, he slowly took a chair and sat in front of my desk. "I had time to read the letter you placed on my desk. While I'm sorry for your illness, I must admit it isn't easy for me to let you go on leave for six months. Please, try to understand my point," he added.

With a nod, I tried to get some clarity in my thoughts. "Of course, it might be difficult, but I'd appreciate it if you'd find a way to help me out. It would make my recovery easier knowing my job was waiting for me when I returned."

He remained quiet for a while, averting his glance from me. "So be it, Ethan," he said abruptly. "Health issues are more important than anything else. If I were in your situation, I'd want the same."

"You mean you'll allow me to take the six-month leave without firing me?" His positive reaction surprised me. I was almost sure he would have opposed my leave.

"Yes. Professionally speaking, I don't have any reason to fire you, and letting you go only based on health problems is illegal." He took a short pause, glancing outside of the window.

"I don't want to find your lawyer in front of my door, ready to send me to Hell. Therefore, you are free to go, but I'd like you to give me a reasonable time before you leave. I mean, don't disappear, please." A smile appeared on his face.

"Of course, I won't. As soon as I have all the details fixed with the doctor, I'll let you know."

Raising his brows, a relieved expression relaxed the features of his face, thankful for having the right time to set up everything before my departure. "That would be helpful, at least to organize who will do your job in the meantime."

"I sincerely appreciate your understanding, and I promise to keep you informed."

He stood from the chair, and without saying anything, he left my office, closing the door behind him.

It was about three o'clock p. m. when my mobile phone rang. "Hello," I said, still focusing on my work.

"Good afternoon. Am I speaking with Mr. Jackson?" a clear, masculine voice asked without introducing himself.

"Yes, that's me. And you are?" suspicion filled my voice.

"This is Professor Jason Doyle. According to Dr. Bernard Wright, you agreed to participate in our research about compulsive liars. Isn't that so?"

When he mentioned Dr. Wright, my expression relaxed, and my doubt faded away. "Yes. In fact, I still can't believe it. I'm grateful to have some confirmation about it. How will everything happen, though? What are the steps I'll have to follow?"

"This is the reason I'm contacting you. It would be good for us to meet. I've been talking with my colleague, but I'd like to have a talk with you and do some further tests, which will be the starting point of our research. We must assess your condition in every single detail; therefore, I'd like to set up an appointment with you. We also need to understand your plans for your trip. Have you thought about your destinations?"

Embarrassed to admit that, with Stewart, I didn't merely think about a destination, but I'd planned the whole journey, I tightened my shoulders. Perhaps it might have been too greedy, thinking about a world tour, but I was so excited that I didn't want to give up such an opportunity.

"Yes, I've got a sort of plan. I hope I haven't shot too high with it."

"We'll talk about it." The amused tone in his voice didn't escape me. "When can you manage to come to the University?"

"I could come right away. My workday is almost finished." I glanced at the clock.

"That would be perfect. Do you know how to reach the University Clinic?"

"Yes, I suppose I can find it."

"Great. You can find me in the Department of Psychiatry and Psychology. You can go to the front desk and tell them you have an appointment with me. I'll come to pick you up," he instructed, keeping a kind tone of voice. As I was speaking on the phone, I searched on the internet for the directions to reach the clinic in the fastest way. "Thank you. I think I can be there within half an hour or forty-five minutes. See you soon."

"Perfect, I'll be waiting for you."

I switched off the computer and got my coat. At that point, I had no doubts about what was happening to me. With hope that I'd be healed from the lies that had trapped me my entire life, I left the office with a bright smile on my face, heading to the University Clinic. Dr. Wright's presence at the meeting was reassuring. The tests I had to undergo took quite a long time, and most were, in my opinion, unusual to assess mental illnesses. They took blood samples, scanned my whole body through a magnetic resonance device, and did an EEG and ECG.

They gave me questionnaires to fill out about my personality, and we had a clinical interview to better evaluate my condition and understand my problem. I couldn't understand the reason for all those questions. There was a moment when I wondered whether the Professor knew more about me than I could ever know. Thinking about it, I was a bit uncomfortable having someone know what is going on in my mind and in my personal life. However, I understood it was necessary if I wanted to have a chance of regaining control of it.

"So, you also mentioned having a sort of plan for the trip. Can you be more specific? I don't want to be pushy, but we need to get an idea of the money required for this experiment."

"Yes, I have it with me." I searched the pockets of my coat. "Here it is. I was thinking of having a tour around the world. It doesn't have to be so, and I can adjust it in a way that might sound more reasonable." The tone of my voice decreased to a whisper.

Prof. Doyle took the sheet of paper, then with a chuckle, he passed it to Dr. Wright. "What do you say?"

Dr. Wright looked carefully at it and smiled. "Next time I need a vacation, I'll have to remember to ask for your help. This sounds like a great world tour."

Averting my gaze from them, I squeezed in my shoulders. I was too demanding when planning my trip, and that was also Stewart's fault, who didn't help in that sense. Nevertheless, it was the vacation of a lifetime, and maybe it was worth making a fool out of myself.

"I don't know what to say, but I'm ready to change my proposal according to the fund. Perhaps I've been naive to plan something when I had no idea about the money at my availability."

Dr. Wright smiled kindly at me. "Don't worry. It's normal to grab the chance of a vacation. The fault was ours because we should have told you about the budget. However, there isn't any given budget, and we need to submit the request to the committee and wait for their opinion. You haven't done anything wrong or stupid. You did what you believed was right, and in your place, we all would have done the same."

The tone of his voice and his words calmed the turmoil of my embarrassment. Of course, anybody would have acted the same way I did. The proof was that Stewart, who was the lead player in the planning of the trip, let himself go as well.

"I still have one question, though." I needed to clear all my doubts, and this was the best time to do so. "How will everything work?"

"Oh, yes, you have to fill out those papers. But we're not in a hurry. You can bring them home and return them to me whenever you can. They are nothing else but the bureaucratic steps to allow you access to the funding, which must be approved by the research committee. As soon as I have them, I'll submit them. We'll inform you when we're ready," Dr. Wright asserted.

"I talked to my supervisor today, and he didn't seem eager to have me away from the job for half a year. I promised to give him time to arrange a temp before I go."

"Of course, I understand. Hmm..." Prof. Doyle mumbled, thinking for a moment. "In the best case, I'd say everything will be set to start in about three months. You might tell him you will leave in four or five months, just to be generous with the timetable."

"I guess that would be a reasonable time. I'll inform him first thing in the morning," I considered, hoping the proposed timeframe would be okay for my supervisor as well.

Then I left the room, ready to go home.

CHAPTER 4

- In the room between Dr. Wright and Prof. Doyle
-

After a long pause of silence, Prof. Doyle glanced at Dr. Wright. "What do you think about him?"

"He'll be the right person for the project. This time, I'm quite sure we'll have another positive result."

Prof. Doyle kept quiet for a few moments, thinking, then shook his head. He picked up the file containing all the tests they performed that day. "I still have some doubts about him. On the other hand, we must test our treatment, especially after the recent modifications we made to it."

"Everything will be fine. I'm positive about his potential. And without testing, we can't reach the desired outcome."

"Hmm... yes, perhaps you're right," Prof. Doyle mumbled. "I have to go through those calculations carefully. I can calibrate the dosage of the drugs he's going to take during the period. Although we need to find a way to shorten the time. Six months is too long. We should get results within one month or a couple of days."

"That's true, but perhaps we might consider shortening the time right away with this patient. We must figure out a solution," Dr. Wright proposed. "What if one of us goes with him?"

Prof. Doyle glanced through narrowed eyelids at him. "You mean to follow him closer?"

"Right. What do you think?"

"That might be a great idea. We need to plan the way we're going to act. He should never be aware that one of us is following him."

CHAPTER 5

The sun had set by the time I reached home.

I was exhausted, and almost mechanically, without even thinking about what I was doing, I poured some food for Moses. The idea that people who can understand my problem are not interested in having any kind of relationship with me, felt disheartening. Excluding a few friends, I considered myself quite lonely.

Moses had been my companion for seven years since the day I found him as a tiny kitten in the middle of the street. From that day on, he behaved like the most loyal of friends. He was the only one who wouldn't care if I wasn't perfect.

It was September when my phone rang once again. I recognized the telephone number of Prof. Doyle.

"Hello," I answered matter-of-factly.

"Good morning, Mr. Jackson. This is Prof. Doyle. Am I disturbing you?"

"No, you're not. Is there any news?" I was still looking at my computer.

"I called to inform you that the plan you have submitted to us was accepted. I hope you have told your supervisor about it, because the time is right, my friend," he said in a happy tone.

For the first time in my entire life, luck found me, and I was thrilled.

"I've got to admit I forgot about it, but this is, indeed, good news." I pushed my chair away from the desk.

"Yes. Is it possible for you to come this afternoon to settle all the details before your departure? Dr. Wright is coming at about five, and if you can join us, we might go over everything at once," he suggested.

"That would be perfect. See you later, then." I could barely keep myself from laughing. Telling my boss about my departure months ago was a smart move, as now I only had to confirm the approaching date.

At ten-to-five, I reached the University Clinic, with my hands shaking and damp with sweat. Every step I took meant an increase in my heartbeat. Useless were all the efforts to hide my excitement; my ear-to-ear grin betrayed me.

Despite my inner turmoil, I tried not to reach Prof. Doyle's office too much in advance. I didn't want to look too eager; although, defining my state of mind as eager didn't give justice to that storm of sensations inside me.

Hesitatingly, short-breathed and with an uncontrollable light shake of my hands, I knocked on his door, trying to regain some calm, drawing a deep breath.

For the next two hours, we talked in a relaxed tone about the plan I had and the technical details. In the beginning, I was a bit shy about it; I was afraid I was shooting too high, with traveling all around the world at their expense. Nevertheless, the fund was incredibly generous, and even my ambitious proposal could fit in.

"So, let's go through the plan again." Dr. Wright tried to keep focused on the aspects of the journey. "This is the camera you will have to wear every single moment of the day. You can put it wherever you want as long as it will never leave your body."

He handed me the camera disguised as a pin. If I hadn't known about it, I'd have never suspected it to be a hidden camera.

"I'll always keep it with me. You can be sure about it." I went through all the duties I needed to fulfill during the journey. "I'll keep a daily diary, and I'll submit it to you every evening."

"Exactly. And every Saturday, we'll send you the corrected version, which you will have to go through, focusing on any differences. We'll also give you some tests to be done on the weekend," Prof. Doyle continued.

"One more thing we need from you." Dr. Wright handed me a small package. "This contains some drugs you will have to take during the whole period..."

"Hold on." I was alarmed. "You never talked about having to take any sort of drugs. That wasn't part of the original deal."

"Don't be afraid. This is part of the treatment and it isn't dangerous. I'm a doctor, and I'd never put the life of my patients in danger. This will help you focus your attention and is nothing that hasn't yet been tested."

I wasn't reassured by his explanation; I've always been reluctant to take medication, and based on their reaction, my hesitation was more than evident.

"Please, let me explain to you how this drug works." He handed me one of the packages. "Those are the same drugs I prescribe to people who have difficulty in focusing on their tasks. It has been on the market for a long time, and you are not the first one to test it."

I looked at the small box and opened one of them to read the leaflet. Indeed, the description confirmed Dr. Wright's words. My only concern was they'd never mentioned this detail.

"For the success of the therapy, we need your full commitment and focus on your task. This isn't just a vacation, even if you are going to travel the world. You committed to participate in this research, and the failure or success depends mostly on your adherence to it," Prof. Doyle explained.

The way he put it made much more sense. Once again, I regretted my doubts and considered my behavior pretty childish. I pursed my lips as I handed them back the package.

A deep sigh escaped my mouth. "You're right. I'm sorry. I was so caught up in the excitement of this adventure that I forgot your reasons. You are doing your job, and I'm thinking about the fun part of it."

Unable to overcome my shame, I shook my head, lowering my gaze to look at my feet, trying to find the right words to apologize. "Please accept my apologies. I'll take those drugs, following your instructions."

Dr. Wright smiled. "You don't need to be sorry. We do understand we should have been clearer about the drugs we're prescribing."

We went through all the details, then I left, ready to pack my bags, including everything I needed to go through my therapy.

For the next three weeks, I didn't receive any news from Dr. Wright, nor Prof. Doyle. I was almost afraid to call them because I feared that if I pissed them with my requests, they might lose their patience and withdraw their offer. Perhaps they would try to find another person who was less demanding than me.

On Friday, Dr. Wright called me, asking if I'd received their email. I was surprised because I didn't receive anything at all.

"Could you check your spam folder?"

"Sure. Hold on a second. I'll do it right away." I checked my email once again. "Well, what do you know? Here's an email from Prof. Doyle. He sent it a couple of days ago, and it passed undetected."

I opened it. Inside were the airline tickets I requested and the hotel reservations, and the land transportation for the first part of the trip.

"So, everything is set. I suppose you can leave and start this adventure," his cheerful voice reached my ears.

The first flight was scheduled in two weeks, and the adrenaline rush started to kick in. I felt lightheaded.

"Yes. Thank you. So far, I haven't had any occasion to use my passport." My voice was only a whisper.

"Well, this is your big chance. Did you take all the necessary vaccinations?"

With a fast nodding of my head, I replied. "Yes. That was one of the first things I had taken care of before I forgot about it."

"Well, then there's nothing else left but to wish you a pleasant and safe trip. Remember to submit a daily diary to us, to keep the mobile phone switched on constantly, and have the camera always with you. See you in half a year."

"Sure. Bye." I printed all the travel documentation, then I went to give the final confirmation to my boss. Walking through the corridor, I could hardly suppress that little voice in the back of my head, whispering the possibility that the cure to my problem could be worse than the illness itself. Something wasn't right, and uncertainty grabbed my soul, trying to stop every step that would bring me closer to falling into a trap.

CHAPTER 6

As a first-time traveler, I decided to go to the airport early to make sure everything would go smoothly. If I got bored, it was better than being in a terrible hurry with the fear of not making it to the gate.

As soon as I arrived, I called Prof. Doyle to check on the functioning of my camera.

"Hello," his busy voice reached me through the telephone.

"Good afternoon. This is Ethan Jackson. I called you because I'm at the airport, and I'm wondering whether everything is working fine. I'd like you to check the camera." I continued to walk along the gates' area.

"Good afternoon, Mr. Jackson. Of course. This is a brilliant idea. Hold on for a second, so I can connect my computer to it." He paused. "Yes, it works perfectly. It's recording every move you make. How do you feel?"

41

"A bit excited, but I think that's normal." I had butterflies in my stomach. "As I reach the hotel, I'll submit the first entry in my trip diary."

"And remember, you are not going to take any notes during the day," he recommended. "You must write everything in the evening, according to your memories about the day you have had. This is important to estimate how your mind can recall and reconnect facts, places, and people."

"Sure. If there are problems with the camera, you can contact me at this number. It will always be on. Let's hope I'll have a strong signal whenever you need to call me," I added.

"Perfect. Have a safe trip, then."

"Thank you. Bye." I ended the call with a relieved exhale.

The first location on my list was Morocco, in Africa. I was afraid my enthusiasm would prevent me from falling asleep during the flight. However, whether it was my excitement tiring me, or the late hour, as soon as the lights on the plane started to fade, my eyes closed.

The next day, in the afternoon, I arrived at my destination: Casablanca. A first glance, it seemed like I'd landed on another planet. Everything was different: exotic and breathtaking.

I was afraid that once the journey ended, I was going to miss the places I'd visit during these months.

Soon after the check-in at the hotel, I decided to check the Wi-Fi in my room was working. After that, I went to explore the city, looking around with the excitement of a little child. I was looking at the world with brand-new eyes.

After my first stroll in the old Medina, I stopped at one of the many restaurants. One of the servers guided me to a table, and as I sat down, I was offered the menu.

To be honest, I couldn't make up my mind what I wanted to have, as I couldn't figure out what would come to my table with any of those exotic dishes.

"Okay, I'll close my eyes and let destiny decide for me." Shutting my eyelids, I allowed my finger to cruise over the menu until I stopped it.

I opened my eyes and tried to make sense of the dish by its name. Nothing came to my mind, but as the server arrived, I ordered what destiny selected and a glass of wine. He took a swift glance at the list and disappeared without saying anything.

Acknowledging the heat of the hot midday sun, I went to the restroom to get refreshed. The weather was pleasantly warm, despite being winter. Back home, I would have wrapped myself in a thick scarf before thinking of leaving the house.

Surprise left me open-mouthed when I returned, and my table was full of small dishes. Confused, I turned around to understand whether I had ordered a portion to be shared with four people, or I'd sat down at another table.

A double check was a must, and everything confirmed that it was my place, but something didn't fit with the amount of food. I called the server.

"Excuse me, but is this what I asked for?" I asked, feeling like the biggest idiot in the world.

"Yes, is there anything wrong?" he wondered with a slightly perplexed expression on his face.

"Was it supposed to be a plate shared with more than one person?" My tone of voice lowered to a hardly audible whisper.

"No, this is a single meal. Look, here at the center, it's what you ordered, and it comes with a selection of side dishes." The server pointed at the different bowls placed in order on the table.

"I see. Is this how people eat in Morocco? Please, excuse my ignorance, but it's quite a lot, and I probably won't be able to finish it." I wasn't sure whether I should apologize for leaving the meal half-consumed.

"Well, this would be what people eat during the holidays or when they are gathered together for parties, but not in normal everyday life."

"So, this means every time I go to a restaurant, I have to expect to have this kind of portion?" I wanted to make sense out of the confusion.

"That's right, but don't worry; you don't have to finish everything." With a chuckle, he left.

Once again, I looked back at my table and slowly started to eat what was offered to me. I must be honest about one thing; the food was a real experience.

Never in my life, have I savored anything like that. The pungent flavor of ginger blended perfectly with cumin and cinnamon in the lamb dish. The juiciness of the meat met the creaminess of the sauce in a perfect wedding. Many other flavors I couldn't recognize, but distinctly they came to revive my senses after the long walk.

The desire to try everything and the limited space in my belly clashed in a titanic battle, having the latter lose over the taste.

I wanted to fix in my mind everything to keep the memory always with me, or until the next meal.

After lunch, I resumed my wanderings, following every street, looking behind every corner, exploring every little particular detail of that beautiful new world.

Every street, bazaar, and shop were like a discovery. I couldn't think about focusing on a single detail.

I wondered how I'd ever be able to describe in my journal what I saw and experienced; it was almost impossible.

However, with the passing of days, this became an easy task, and writing in my diary became a routine.

The first month on the road brought me to discover Africa, and I realized how different every country was.

Nevertheless, with the discovery of the world, came the disappointment, when I appreciated how far the version of the facts I submitted diverged from the ones recorded by the camera. It was like comparing the records of two people traveling in different countries.

The most striking revelation was that in Morocco, I hadn't been to the main Bazaar. I just walked some small markets, but nothing to do with the one I described in my diary. Also, the description of my first lunch wasn't correct. The meal I was offered was abundant, but not like the four-person portion I reported. At least one minor divergence faulted every memory, and in some cases, they were significant issues.

Disappointment literally crushed my self-confidence, and I wanted to give up everything, reconsidering my whole life and memories. *What is real and what isn't in everything I remember about my life?* - I shook my head in disbelief. What gave me strength were the evening chats with Stewart, who encouraged me not to quit.

The first big change in my nomadic life happened almost immediately after visiting Morocco, when I reached Ghana. The original plan was to book all the hotels month by month and choose the way of crossing the border accordingly with what the local tour operator suggested.

As I was looking at the tours offered, I stumbled across a 21-day trip from Ghana to Benin, through Togo. I assumed it could be the best solution to see most of every country, without having to bother about how to cross the frontier each time.

"May I help you?" the receptionist asked as she acknowledged my concerned expression.

"Not quite - I'm not entirely sure," I admitted hesitatingly. "You see, I was planning to travel to Benin, and I've booked and paid in advance for the hotels. However, this kind of tour would give me the chance to see more and ease my trip."

"I can give a call to the agency that's organizing this tour. Perhaps they can help you find a solution. The agent is regularly coming here to give us the new brochures, or to arrange customized tours for our guests. If you want, I can ask him to contact you directly."

"Please do so. I would love to participate, it seems so interesting."

"If you are spending the day here at the hotel, I might also ask him to come here today," she assured.

"Thank you. I'll spend the rest of the day at the pool. He can find me there."

I took the brochure with me and went to enjoy the sun. After a few hours, a tall man wearing a business suit approached me, introducing himself as the travel agent the receptionist was talking about.

Expressing my interest in participating in the tour, I hoped I was still in time to be part of the group leaving within a couple of days. My only concerns were the reservations I already paid for, and I prayed he could help me.

He remained for a moment, thinking about it. "Well, I think we can arrange a refund, or at least a partial one, with which you can partially pay for this tour. I can't promise you anything. Let me try to contact the hotels you booked to negotiate a solution. Would you give me the booking vouchers?"

His words injected me with hope. Perhaps I was a lucky person. "Of course. If you can wait for a second, I'll go get them, so you can deal with them right away."

He nodded without saying a word, and I rushed to my room to get all the reservations.

As I was getting them from my rucksack, I thought I should call Prof. Doyle to inform him of the change. Perhaps it would be wise if, for the rest of the trip, I took care of the itinerary personally, billing the difference from time to time.

Panting, I returned to the bar, where the travel agent was still waiting for me. "Here are the bookings that have been done so far." I handed him the folder.

"Perfect. I'll try to contact the hotels immediately, and I'll inform you about the response. You can continue to relax and enjoy your holiday. I'll take charge of everything," he promised with a nod.

We parted, and I called Prof. Doyle, hoping my decision to change the itinerary wasn't a problem. I knew I should have informed him before agreeing on anything with the travel agent, but I was too eager to grab the opportunity.

Once again, luck was on my side since Prof. Doyle didn't have any objections. Nevertheless, the tone of his voice gave me the impression that something wasn't the way it should be.

But we agreed that from that day on, they would give me a sort of monthly allowance based on what I had been spending so far, and if extra money was needed, they would pay it.

Recalling my duty of writing a diary, I decided to have a walk around.

That evening, as I came back from my daily wanderings, the receptionist handed me an envelope with the response of my travel agent.

The eagerness to find out whether he could manage to get the refund was so strong that I opened it without waiting to get to my room.

"Awesome!" I exulted as I realized that I had a partial refund of the bookings. He wrote that if I was still interested, I had to pay the fee for the trip directly to the receptionist.

A wide grin brightened up my face, and I ran as fast as possible to get the money.

After a couple of days, I joined the group of tourists I'd be traveling with for the next twenty-one days. It was comfortable to travel in a group. I got tired of being lonely in my journey to discover the world and myself, and I couldn't fathom what destiny had in store for me.

CHAPTER 7

- Between Dr. Wright and Prof. Doyle after the call with Ethan -

"Dammit, Mr. Jackson, this isn't a vacation," Prof. Doyle's voice trembled as he struggled to remain calm and dial Dr. Wright's number.

"Hello, Jason," Dr. Wright answered, recognizing the number of his colleague.

"I've just received a call from Mr. Jackson, and I guess you know what it's all about, if you've been following what he's been doing." His foot nervously fidgeted as he tried to keep his voice steady.

"Yes, I know, but I don't think that this can bring us any trouble, either with our client, with the timetable or with the fund," he answered, sensing the tense tone in the voice of his colleague. "It indeed forces us to change a few aspects of our schedule, but the fact that he's on a guided tour allows us to predict his movements. As soon as I can speak with our client, I will inform him about this change."

Prof. Doyle shook his head and stood from his chair, nervously pacing around the room. "Honestly, this plan is only making me nervous. Why did we need to have our patient so far away?"

An amused smirk appeared on Dr. Wright's lips. "Come on, Jason, let Mr. Jackson enjoy his vacation while he can. Soon we'll enter the second stage of the treatment, and we have to be sharp. We can't allow these little deviations from the original plan to take our focus off the research."

Prof. Doyle took a deep breath, closing his eyes to focus on his heartbeat. "You're right. We need to stay focused. Let me know if other problems arise with our client, and keep an eye on Mr. Jackson; he appears to be unpredictable."

"I will do that. Take care!" Dr. Wright recommended, ending the call.

Placing his mobile phone back in his pocket, Dr. Wright stared from the tinted window of the private taxi he'd hired.

Indeed, there were details we may have overlooked, but now we must keep on going.

With a light gesture, he prompted the driver to continue his ride.

CHAPTER 8

The first item on the agenda for the day was exploring the city of Accra. Although I'd visited most of it, I didn't complain about this detail.

As we were walking the streets toward an open market, a female voice reached me. "Are you all alone?"

I turned my head to check whether the question was directed at me. A lovely-looking girl with ruffled, curly hair and bright eyes the color of the sky was strolling at my side, waiting for an answer.

"Oh, you were talking to me?"

"So it seems," she replied.

"Yes, I'm traveling alone. What about you? Are you with your boyfriend?"

"I don't have one; I'm still available." She winked. "I'm with my sister," she clarified, pointing her finger to another girl who was looking around the stands in the market.

That answer made me chuckle. For some reason, I was glad she was single, but I was also aware that she wasn't for me. In fact, I was sure I'd have never been able to have another relationship, at least not until my problem was solved.

"My name is Karen. And who are you?"

"I'm Ethan, Ethan Jackson. Nice to meet you." I think I blushed, shaking her hand.

Combing her hair with one hand, she continued, "This is my first time in Africa. I don't have much time to travel for long periods, as my job is taking everything away from me. Still, this time, I absolutely wanted to go somewhere special. My sister is turning thirty next week, and we decided to take this occasion to go on holiday together far away."

"Where do you live?" I tried to guess from her accent.

"I come from Heidelberg, Germany. What about you?" she glanced at me with her bright blue eyes.

"I'm from Boston." In front of those eyes, words were failing me.

"Really? I've always dreamed of visiting the U.S. What does Boston look like?"

"Big and crowded, but it's my home, and people are friendly." I wanted to give the best fitting description of my hometown, even though I was aware, the only way to get to know a city is by living there.

"It seems like a place where you can't find any time to be on your own," she responded, giggling.

"It depends on the neighbors you find. I don't know whether I'm a failure with socialization or not, but I can definitely find places to be alone." I shrugged.

"I do live a bit outside the city, and there, I can find a lot of peace whenever I need it. What I enjoy the most are the long walks in the woods."

"That must be wonderful. What is Germany like?"

"Germany is a great place to live, at least from my point of view. There are big cities like Berlin and Frankfurt, which are the heart of the politics and economy of the country. Although, if you go to smaller places and towns, you might believe you have been brought back in time or to another place. In any case, you always have the chance to reach the woods." She casually played with a string of her purse.

"Sounds like a nice city."

"You should come to visit Germany if you haven't ever been there," she pursued. "Have you been to Africa before?"

"No, this is my first time, although I've been in Africa for about ten days already, and I plan to continue my travels for another six months."

"Wow, half a year?" She goggled at me.

"Well, it isn't what it sounds like. I'm not a rich person taking a tour around the world. I'm on a sort of therapy journey." I wasn't yet ready to reveal more than that.

"Perhaps I'm a bit indiscreet, and you don't have to explain anything, but what kind of therapy? Did you have a burnout?"

"You might call it something like that, even if I don't know how to define it." I tried to be as vague as possible. I don't like those who try to intrude into the lives of other people, but I liked her. Her way of asking personal questions was so innocent that it was difficult to resist.

The girl she told me was her sister came toward us, holding a colorful dress. "What do you think? Would it be the right gift for a middle-aged woman who still looks young?"

With a simple nod, I offered her a smile. "I think it might be appropriate, but it depends on the woman."

"Indeed. By the way, I'm Bettina," she introduced herself, scrutinizing me from head to feet.

"Pleased to meet you. My name is Ethan."

"He's from the States," Karen chirped enthusiastically.

"Don't mind my sister too much. She's crazy for the U.S. I'm not a big fan, but nothing personal, of course. So, where do you live?"

"I live in Boston. Karen had good things to say about Germany, and I'd love to visit it. In fact, I might travel there in the future, and I might need some hints on what I should see," I said.

"This might be your lucky day. I work with a travel agency, and I can help you with that," she offered.

"That would be helpful, but rather than seeing tourist attractions, I'd like to see why Karen loves it so much. I'd like to see both the historical places and natural beauties. Also, I'm interested in the everyday lives of people living there."

"Well, this is my card. No need to book any tour, but we can stay in touch by email. I can help you whenever possible," she said.

I took the business card she gave me and placed it in the pocket of my shirt. "Thank you, I appreciate it."

As she left to join her sister, I started to focus on the details of the market, and so far, nothing impressed me. To be honest, I was intrigued by Karen. I couldn't stop following her with my eyes. I tailed every move she made, and every time she laughed, I felt dangerously attracted to her.

"Now, Ethan, you need to concentrate on your therapy. You are not here to have fun with the first girl within your reach. Besides, she isn't for you," my voice of reason kept saying.

In the evening, we reached our first destination, and with that, our hotel, close to the border with Togo. We got the keys to our rooms, but I didn't have the time to have a shower and write something about my day in the diary. It was almost time for dinner, but I felt so tired I was sure I wouldn't have anything to say if I wrote it later.

I had switched off my laptop when I heard someone knocking at my door. Without asking who it was, I opened the door, and I remained speechless when I saw Karen smiling at me.

"You will miss dinner!" she yelped.

Grimacing, I peered at her, as I was sure it was too early. "What time is it?"

"It's half past seven. Come; everybody is waiting for you."

Grabbing the room key, I rushed out with her. "My clock must be broken," I apologized, looking at my wristwatch.

She smiled and turned her gaze away from me, still pulling me by the hand.

Without even thinking, following only my instinct, I did something I was afraid I would regret for the rest of my life. With a swift move, I pulled her toward me, and as we faced each other, I held her tightly to myself and kissed her.

"ETHAN, STOP IT, GODDAMMIT!" a voice yelled from the back of my head.

I decided to ignore it. The feeling of her body against mine and the taste of her lips made me forget about my irresponsible and unacceptable behavior. I knew she would soon pull away and slap me for being such a brute, but I couldn't resist.

However, as much as I was enjoying kissing her– and at the same time, waiting for her violent reaction– I realized she was returning my kiss.

Not only did she return it, but she grabbed my hair, pulling me closer and closer, pushing me against the wall.

I loved it!

Time seemed to stop in that interminable kiss, careless about being spotted by anyone passing by. Then, she suddenly parted. "Dinner!" she yelled.

Trying to understand what she was saying, I remained frozen for a moment, but then, I realized all the others were probably waiting for us.

With a quick kiss on her forehead, I smiled. "We'll talk later, then." I was amused, as we walked to the restaurant.

"Meet me at eleven, here in the hall," she proposed before we entered the room.

With a broad grin, I nodded. Then the reason for my journey returned to my mind, and the first problem arose like a ghost from the mist. *How am I going to explain this to Dr. Wright and Prof. Doyle? What will they say? I can't lie about it;* they *have it on camera.*

At that point, I wasn't concerned about the possibility of quitting my trip, but about the fact that my therapy would end too.

I need to get cured from my habit. I need to fix my problem. Despair grabbed my soul as my hands started to shake, fearing I had to quit not only the therapy but also my new relationship with Karen.

Later in the evening, as agreed, we met in the hall.

"Hello," I whispered shyly.

"Hi, there." She beamed.

For an interminable number of seconds, neither of us had anything to say. It was like we couldn't speak anymore.

Reaching for her hand, I gently held it in mine, and a smile appeared on my face at that touch. Like the screeching sound of nails on a chalkboard, I recalled the reason I was on vacation.

It was time to be completely honest with her. She had the right to know about my mental condition, and regardless of how difficult it was, I tried my best to explain everything. Too many people had suffered because of my lying behavior, and I didn't want to add more victims to the count.

"Ethan..." she whimpered after a long pause. "I don't know what to say. Are you telling me you are a pathological liar, and I should believe in this story?"

"It sounds crazy, I know, but I can show it to you. There are all the emails I've exchanged with my psychiatrist. Also, I should still have a copy of the letter he wrote to my employer." I was desperate to explain to her my situation. "I'm a liar, but this time, I'm telling you the truth. I might scramble the events in my head, but I'll never tell a lie about my feelings, and I'd never lie when I say that, since we met, I can't stop thinking about you."

We reached my room, where I could show her everything I had. She took a seat at the chair in front of the writing table and went through all the documentation. As she finished reading everything, she raised her gaze to me and smiled. "You told the truth. Can we say you are not a complete liar?"

Relieved, my expression relaxed, and I felt as if a stone had fallen from my heart. "At least you can be sure I'm not a jerk."

"That is the most important thing for me, the knowledge that you will never hurt me on purpose. No one is perfect, and I think it's an excellent starting point that you are trying so hard to find a solution to your problem."

She stood from the chair and held me tightly, kissing me softly. I wasn't in love with her; I was crazy about her.

When she parted from me, I felt like I was missing something special and felt lost. "Can you stand it?"

"It's too early to think about it. We'll see what happens during these three weeks," she suggested, lowering her gaze.

Glancing at the clock, I moaned. "We need to go to sleep, or we'll never wake up in time tomorrow."

I hoped falling in love with Karen wasn't the only positive news and that more would come.

We planned to meet again and see whether there was a chance for our newborn relationship. I needed to believe in that dream. It was something that made me feel alive like I hadn't felt for a long time.

The following day, we reached the border with Togo. We had an endless car ride, but I slept for the whole trip, forgetting to notice anything except my dreams. I woke up just for the formalities at the border for the passport control, falling asleep immediately after, as we resumed our road trip.

"Wake up, sleeping beauty. We arrived at the camp." A voice interrupted my slumber as its owner shook me.

I opened one eye, and it took some seconds to open the other. "Where are we?"

"We're in the Mount Klouto Region," Janet, one of the other tourists in the group, explained.

I felt dizzy and in need of a massage, but I tried to wake up to notice everything about the place, so I'd have something to write in my diary. Thankfully, the following day, I'd be free to explore the natural beauty of the site and perhaps to have a visit to the village.

For once, we were free from a set schedule. Not every tour was mandatory, and it meant I could plan my exploration and wandering in freedom.

Something I started to dislike was the arranged tours to the villages or to the slums. It made me feel like an idiot going to the zoo to look at the wild animals kept in captivity, far from their natural environment, for humans' amusement. What was worse, in this case, was that they weren't poor animals to be looked at; they were people like us, not a circus attraction.

For this reason, I decided to skip that part and to focus on the scenery and Karen.

She brought to my life a breath of fresh air. I wasn't trying to notice and concentrate on what happened during the day anymore. I was enjoying it, and I hoped it would make a difference in the diary.

We did all the things young couples do when traveling together; we laughed, took funny pictures, and exchanged tenderness. I told her about my life and about Moses, and I warned her that not everything might have been true.

"This is the first time a man tells me he might have told some lies. Generally, they lie to impress me." She lowered her gaze to look at our hands, fingers entwined. "At least I know if I find out you were telling lies, I can't blame you, as you warned me."

"Despite my lying problem, I want to be honest with you. Before I knew about my disease, I made too many people suffer, and I don't want to do the same to you."

"You won't. I'm taking my own risks."

Days went by, and I spent the time amazed at the wonderful places we visited, the different cultures, and the people we met. We drove all through Togo to Benin, crossing the Tata Somba region, staying in an Eco-lodge, learning from the locals about their lifestyles, comparing it unavoidably with ours.

On the eleventh day of our journey, Sunday, arrived. Keeping my eyes closed, I clicked on the document, trying to find a good time to check the results.

I opened one eye, but not being able to see it right, I also opened the other. The corrected parts appeared to be slightly less, and I wondered whether it was because of Karen, or because the therapy had started to bear fruit.

Carefully, I went through the entire document.

With a pleased smile, I acknowledged we had a scheduled visit to the slums, and I decided not to go to join them. It was also true that I walked the whole time with Karen, taking funny pictures with her camera. And I told the truth when I stated that I felt so tired that I fell asleep during our road trip to the Mount Klouto region. However, there were still a lot of red marks, and I hoped they would consistently decrease week after week.

Those red-marked corrections told me I didn't walk on my own at nighttime, as it was forbidden to leave the premises of the lodge because of the wild animals.

Again, I was disappointed there weren't any elephants crossing the property, but it was a few hundred meters away.

Perhaps the therapy had started to yield some results, and I wouldn't lie anymore, or at least I'd only lie when I wanted, and not because of a fault in my brain.

Nevertheless, it made me wonder, and I began to be curious about the difference between the old diaries and the most recent ones. I opened the old documents, those I submitted before dating Karen.

"That can't be true!"

Going through the previous versions, I counted all the markings: 2,400 corrections in 3,000 words, which is to say eighty percent of what I wrote was a lie. "Damn! I remembered them being a bit less. My brain has been messing around with truth and lies again."

Then, I went to take account of the ones in the most recent diary: 1,000 out of 4,120.

Four times, I calculated them and put them down on a separate piece of paper. Placing a sign for every red marking, I counted them, writing down their number.

My brain wasn't messing with me this time. I began with eighty percent being lies and ended with twenty percent. It was surreal. I could almost have said that I made it, and I was more willing to do the tests they sent along with the corrections.

***

Most of the following day was spent driving through Benin. The journey wasn't comfortable, as the road seemed like it had been paved a long time ago, but never maintained. The red sand covering the holes created a deceiving effect of continuity, which was uncovered as soon as the car drove over them. Despite this detail, I was able to fall asleep, forgetting about the diary I was supposed to write in the evening.

The challenge in driving on that terrain wasn't only the stress posed on the car's suspension, but also trying to avoid bigger holes and other vehicles coming from the other direction. Many times, we had to slow down because some street merchants stopped the passing cars to sell fruits or bread. This was rather common to see while driving in Africa; it was also a way to do the groceries. Frankly, besides the fact that the trip gets slowed down, it's quite a straightforward way to buy.

What attracted my attention the most was the beauty of the rich, red sand, and the colorful places we drove through. I thought I could fall in love with that vibrant scenery.

Like a memento, I couldn't stop thinking that soon, Karen would have to return to Germany, and I'd have to resume my trip alone. Would we still be able to chat and call each other? Would our relationship end, and we'd go on with our lives as if nothing had ever happened? I didn't want to think about it. I was falling in love with her, and whether she was supposed to be the love of my life or a vacation fling, I wanted to live it intensely.

**

In the evening, walking beside Karen, was almost like I could hear her thoughts and concerns; they resembled mine. "What will happen in six days?" she asked suddenly.

Startling at the sound of her voice, I didn't have any answers to offer her – a lump formed in my throat, impeding me from making any sound.

Tears welled up in my eyes at the idea of saying goodbye, and I hate goodbyes.

"Supposedly, we'll go on different paths, but I don't want to give up on our feelings." My voice was a raspy whisper, filled with pain and fear. "We need to try, at least until we know what we feel for each other. Being apart can help us in this way," I tried to rationalize, but I knew I was lying to her and to myself.

She stopped and locked her eyes on mine. "You don't believe a single word you are saying, do you?"

I felt like a child caught stealing jam from the kitchen.

"Karen, this isn't about what I do or don't believe; this is about what I feel, and I don't want to give up our relationship so easily. I want to give us a chance, and that's what I'm going to do from this day on."

She lowered her gaze. "I'm sorry. Perhaps, I'm overreacting, and I'm also afraid of what will happen to us."

That night, exactly as all the following nights, we had sex, regardless of whether my psychiatrist would know about it or not. Those were the times we needed to connect intimately, never to let go.

No words could ever describe the feeling of making love to her, the perfection of our bodies fusing together to create one, a perfect one. Those were the moments when I forgot I was in therapy, and that every single thing was recorded on camera. There wasn't any doctor or professor, and most important of all, there were no lies. In my considerations, I wondered whether this would have counted as an improvement from the point of view of my psychiatrist.

I didn't have much time to get in touch with Stewart, and I hoped I wasn't going to hurt his feelings by ignoring him. However, it was true, and I didn't have time to do anything else. All I wanted was to use that part of the trip exclusively to strengthen the bond with Karen, writing in my daily diary, and traveling. It was quite a hectic period.

It's so crazy to think that I almost miss my boring life in Boston, I thought, amused.

Everything was reported, from the visit to the intense, emotional "slave route" in Benin to the Temple of the Python, the snake sacred to the Dangbè deity in Togo, and to Togoville, which was considered the heart of the voodoo culture. The fetish market and the visit to the voodoo doctor, where we received our blessings according to their beliefs.

The last day, I went to the airport with Karen and her sister, Bettina. I was supposed to leave later, but I wanted to stay with her for as long as possible. We exchanged all our contact information, from chat to email, telephone numbers to home addresses. We decided we'd do everything to keep our relationship alive until my therapy came to an end. After that, we'd figure out a way to build a life together.

I knew it wouldn't be easy, and I was afraid we couldn't keep up a long-distance relationship, particularly given my mental illness.

As Bettina went to take care of other business, we were left alone, trying to find the right words.

"This isn't a goodbye, Ethan," she said, her voice trembling.

In the desperate attempt to find something to say, I held her tightly to me, but everything that came to my mind sounded empty. After all, what could I say that would have even been the truth?

My heart sank, and tears welled up in my eyes.

"Karen, I don't want to be far from you, not even for one day," I started to say, hoping not to break into tears. "I've never felt like this with any other woman."

"Those are exactly my same feelings, Ethan. We'll see what is destined for us. Maybe it wouldn't have been a bad idea to try one of those voodoo practices." She tried to smile.

"If only there was a chance it would have worked. Unfortunately, from what I saw, it was only mumbo-jumbo...nothing to do with something real."

Heartbroken, I watched her go to the safety check. I still had to wait one hour for my check-in booth to open.

A painful whimper escaped my mouth. *This isn't going to be easy.*

CHAPTER 9

As I feared, parting from Karen was one of the most challenging tasks in my life. But for the sake of an eventual future together, I needed to continue my therapy.

Therefore, my journey went on without her, but we kept chatting in the evenings.

In December, I reached Johannesburg, South Africa. It was the first time I spent Christmas away from my family. It was also the first time for me to experience summer in December.

Day after day my performance kept improving, and my diary started to resemble the version recorded by the camera.

One day, my telephone rang unexpectedly. "Good morning, Mr. Jackson," Dr. Wright greeted. "Or better, good afternoon, as you should have had your lunch."

"Good morning to you, too. Yes, I had my lunch a few minutes ago. Now, I'm trying to get back to my hotel."

"I'm calling you to talk about this girl you met on the previous leg of the journey," he began, introducing the reason for his call.

"You mean Karen?" As he mentioned her, my mouth fell open.

"Yes. You had a sort of romantic relationship for three weeks. I was wondering what your state of mind is now that you have resumed your 'solo' trip."

"Without her, I'm lonelier, and I miss her," I whined, visually touring the surroundings. "I'm not sure whether I love her or not. After all, we spent too short a period together to be sure about my feelings, but..."

No words could explain to him what I was feeling, because I couldn't describe it to myself.

"I don't want to be nosy about your personal issues. My questions are not meant to be indiscreet. Nevertheless, I'd like to be aware of every change in your life, to understand better the trigger to fix your lying behavior."

"I'd like to be able to comprehend it myself, too. She came into my life like a storm, and when I told her I was a pathological liar, she didn't judge me. She accepted the fact that I'm not perfect, and she has to take my words with the right amount of doubt," I admitted. "She's another incentive to get rid of my problem. I want to have an honest relationship with her, although honesty isn't the only issue we're facing. She's living too far from me."

"That might be an interesting point. Have you ever fallen in love with someone before?" he asked. "Did you feel the same for the other former girlfriends as you do for this one? Have you ever desired to get deeper into the reason for your behavior for the sake of your relationship with any of them?"

For a moment, I remained silent to think about his questions. Perhaps this was the first time I felt that way. With all the other relationships, I failed because I wasn't in love with them. Maybe I didn't care about being a better person for the sake of the other girls.

We had a long talk, a sort of psychoanalytic session by phone. My confidence level about my therapy was getting higher and higher. It made me feel like I could return home as a new man – a man who had full control of whether I was telling a lie or the truth.

I looked at the clock; it was 3:30 P.M. During the call, I hadn't thought of what to say in my diary. However, besides the lousy public transportation, the city was kept clean. It didn't resemble the other countries I'd previously visited at all.

At about five, I reached the hotel, with the clear idea of having been robbed by the taxi driver. I came in disappointed and not willing to go anywhere the day after. In fact, I was ready to leave the city and even the entire country if that was the case.

With a lazy movement, I opened my laptop and started to write in my diary. I had no idea where I got the inspiration from, but suddenly, a lot of details of the day appeared in front of my eyes. All I had to do was to describe those images.

I hoped they were more genuine than the previous ones and I could tell a more truthful version of the day I had.

As soon as I didn't have anything else to write, I submitted it, hoping to receive positive feedback. I switched to chat, but this time, I only wanted to talk with Karen. Therefore, I set my profile as invisible, and I called her.

We had a long conversation. When I saw her on my screen, my loneliness disappeared, and she was the one I needed in my everyday life.

Nevertheless, I was afraid the day would come when only seeing her wouldn't be enough anymore. I was scared from that moment on there would be some decisions to be made, and perhaps we would have to split.

Time went by, and after a couple of days, I arrived in Cape Town at the International Airport. After gathering my luggage, I started to walk toward the exit, searching for a taxi.

"Good evening." I approached one of the drivers.

"Good evening. Where can I drive you to?"

I took out the address of the hotel I'd printed. The name of the street was quite challenging for me to pronounce, and I was afraid I'd say the wrong address.

The taxi driver examined the piece of paper I gave him and nodded.

"How much will it cost?"

"That will be 260 Rand," he responded without even turning to look at me.

I had no idea how far the hotel was, but it seemed to me a bit expensive. That was something like 26 U.S. dollars, but at that time of the day, it might have been the only choice, so without reply, I got in and tried to relax.

The weather worsened as we reached the city. The wind was blowing, as if there was a storm approaching.

I hoped there wasn't a hurricane coming through, but if that were the case, we should have been informed about it upon our arrival. Also, I considered that the airplane would have had some trouble landing.

We arrived at the hotel, and I struggled to reach reception with the luggage.

"Is this typical weather in Cape Town?" I questioned as I approached the desk, handing the receptionist my passport.

"Cape Town is a windy city because of the mountains. You can expect this kind of wind going on for many days."

"Is there any weather bulletin?" I asked curiously.

"The forecast promised the wind should cease in the next couple of days, and generally, they are right. You are going to stay here for about a week?"

"Yes, that's the plan." I was wondering whether I should trust them or not.

"Then you might get the chance to experience a less windy city and have a pleasant trip to Table Mountain."

"That's what I hope." I shook my head as I got the key.

I reached my room and looked out the window. The wind blew so violently it seemed as if it was going to eradicate all the trees and houses, delivering them somewhere else– maybe even in the middle of the sea.

In my life, I had never experienced violent storms, and this one was quite scary, or perhaps I was overreacting.

It took exactly three days for the wind to become mild enough to allow me to try to have a ride with the funicular to the top of the mountain. When I arrived there, I realized I wasn't the only one who had been waiting for the weather to calm down. Considering the queue, I decided to give up. I reached a secondary road which could lead me there in three hours of walking.

Most of all, I was interested in taking pictures of the scenery and having a hike in nature.

The weather was pleasant, and the gentle breeze made my walk easy to endure. Despite this, I didn't reach the top of the mountain, because my legs were already like wet spaghetti at the halfway point. Glancing at the valley behind me, I sat down on a rock and enjoyed the view in silence.

Nobody else but me was there, as most people wouldn't have liked to take such a challenging way. Only an occasional hiker passed me by, and I was at peace with myself and with the world. Contemplating the scenery and enjoying the inner serenity in my heart, I lost track of time. As a result, it was dark by the time I arrived at the hotel.

On the last day in Cape Town, I decided to have another walk around the city.

I reached the "long street," and I was enchanted by the way it looked. It featured old, colonial-style buildings, but with a modern twist. Invited by those colorful buildings, I went to sit down in one of the terraces and had a beer as I followed what was going on down on the streets.

Something I noticed then was all the customers were white people, not necessarily tourists, but no black people. Then, I looked around more closely, and besides the few kids working as servers to get some extra cash during the study period, the rest of the personnel in restaurants and pubs were black.

Considering 32 percent of the population was white, I deemed it strange. Probably, the apartheid lived still, and Nelson Mandela's effort didn't reach the goal he had in mind, as Cape Town was still a city ran by whites and worked by blacks.

My telephone started to ring. I looked at it, and I was surprised to see Karen's number.

"Hello, babe."

"Hi, Ethan..." Her voice was sad. "I just... I don't know why I called you now, without waiting for our chat this evening."

"We don't need an appointment to call each other."

"Of course not, but I had a conversation with your psychiatrist; a certain Dr. Wright, isn't he?"

I wondered why he'd called her. Our relationship was none of his business. Although I was his patient, there must be a line beyond which my private life didn't concern him at all.

Recalling the phone call I'd had with him, I started to fear he asked her to end our relationship.

"Karen..."

"No, let me finish." Her voice toughened. "We had quite a long talk, and he explained to me the effect of our relationship on your therapy."

"He shouldn't intrude in my private life, much less in yours."

"That's what I thought too, but on the other hand, you started a critical journey, and you need to focus on that." Her voice was trembling as if she was close to crying.

"Karen, please. I love you..."

"I love you, too, Ethan, but think about it. How could we build our relationship if you don't focus on treating your illness? I accept you as the person you are, but you realize if you don't get better, it would be frustrating for both of us. This is not a way to quit, but perhaps we should talk about this at the end of your therapy. I'll be waiting; it won't be impossible. Besides, we'll have time to consider what our feelings are."

The whole world suddenly lost all its color, and I was forced back to my gray existence, where one day simply followed the other.

Perhaps she was right. It would have been selfish of me to pretend I had her acceptance, knowing how difficult it was to live a life with a man who can't stop telling lies. Friendship is one thing, but having a deeper bond with someone is another. Love is mainly trusting each other, and how could I demand her trust if I couldn't even tell the truth when writing a diary about my day?

"You're right. I understand how frustrating it can be to have a relationship with a person you can't trust. But, I want to change. I don't want to lie anymore, the way I did in the past. I don't want to hurt people around me, and I don't want to be hurt either," I promised, with a lump forming in my throat at the possibility of losing her. "I'll be back for you, and I'll never tell a lie for the rest of my life."

"Then I'll be waiting for you. Whether we're supposed to live together for the rest of our lives or not, I'll be by your side."

"Goodbye, Karen..." Tears collected in my eyes and began to flow in large drops down my cheeks.

"See you soon, Ethan."

That was the most painful goodbye of my whole life.

Although it wasn't a farewell, in my heart, it hurt like the stabbing of a thousand knives. Once again, my lies ruined everything, and I wanted to punch myself.

That evening, I wasn't in the mood to talk to Stewart. I knew he was doing fine with the two lovers. Not even Moses was missing me anymore.

Lazily, I wrote my diary, without trying too hard to recall the events of the day. I wasn't interested anymore in the therapy or even in life.

***

From the moment I was forced to take a break from Karen, the time started to fly away.

The next day, I left South Africa, and I arrived in the evening at the Livingstone airport. It was a small one, as I noticed from the beginning; we could walk from our airplane to the arrival gate.

At first glance, the gate itself looked small. In fact, it was a small lobby at the end of which was the passport control.

Quite minimalist, I thought, but at least not disperse, and hopefully efficient. Patiently, I positioned myself in a queue together with the other passengers of the flight and waited for my turn to get my entry visa. I was making a quick visual tour of the surroundings when I spotted something interesting.

It was an information poster which stated that now it was possible to get the visa for both Zambia and Zimbabwe from the Livingstone airport, for only fifty U.S. dollars.

A real bargain, I thought, and decided for that option, rather than paying the same amount for having the visa only for one country. Somewhere, I read the Victoria Falls were more beautiful and spectacular from the Zimbabwe side, and I didn't want to miss such an opportunity.

The wait was almost endless. Even though the queue wasn't long, the border officers were a bit slow in issuing the visas, and I feared I'd be destined to spend the night in the hall. Eventually, I got the double visa, and then I rushed to the baggage claim, hoping, at least, to have my luggage right away.

Due maybe to the fact that there weren't many passengers with me on the plane, and the air traffic was reduced, I got my luggage in a matter of seconds. Thankful for the news, I walked to the exit.

"Do you need a taxi, Sir?" A man approached me promptly as he saw me coming out.

"I guess so. I need to go to this hotel." I showed the reservation.

He briefly inspected the paper before handing it back to me. "Sure. No problem."

"How much would it be?"

He thought about it for a while. "It's going to be ten dollars," he answered as we paced to the parking lot.

I didn't know whether this was a reasonable price or not. On that occasion, I didn't bargain; I wanted to be sure we agreed beforehand so there wouldn't be any bad surprises when I reached the hotel. The fare seemed to be quite fair, as we drove a long distance to reach the city. Though, when the taxi driver took a secondary and unpaved road, I started to become a little concerned that he didn't understand at all the place where I needed to be.

The sun had already set, and I didn't have any idea where we were, or where he was driving me. Moreover, I didn't dare to ask anything. When we arrived at the hotel and I recognized it from the pictures on the internet, a loud exhale relieved me. I paid the taxi fee and walked to the reception desk, looking around to get familiar with the new environment.

The place was calm, and the only noises were the sounds of nature surrounding the premises. I reached my bungalow, and after a quick tour, I fell in love with it. However, I was quite tired, and I let myself fall on the bed and fell fast asleep. There weren't any alarm clocks or schedules, and what I was going to do during the day was up to me. That was the freedom I was going to miss once I returned home to the old routine. I was supposed to stay for only four days; the last one, I decided to visit the Victoria Falls.

To reach the park, I needed to book a taxi ride, which I did the previous day. Therefore, immediately after breakfast, a driver waited for me at the reception desk.

"So, do you want me to drive you to the Zimbabwe side?"

"Yes, please. I've heard that from there, you'll have a better view of the falls," I replied.

"You heard it right, then. I'm sure you will love it. You see, I'm from Zimbabwe, and I've seen the falls from both sides. Yet, the best way to enjoy them is from that side." He parked in front of the border checkpoint. "Okay, you go through the passport check, and I'll be waiting for you on the other side." He pointed with his finger to the booth of the border control. I reached the queue, filled out the form, and in a matter of minutes, I was in the taxi, going to the entrance.

"Here is the park. When would you like me to come to get you?"

I scratched the back of my head, figuring out a reasonable time. I couldn't tell how long it would take me to visit the whole complex. I was confident I'd find a way to spend my time, so I told him to come to pick me up at about five o'clock. This meant I had five hours to spend there, but I figured I could eat my lunch there. Moreover, I was sure there would be a lot for me to see regarding the natural environment and scenery.

I paid my entrance fee and went in, looking around, when a family of warthog crossed my path. They were quite cute, especially the young ones, and, of course, they deserved to be in my photo album. They were probably used to the presence of tourists because they kept walking among all the other people without much caring about them. Besides the falls, I had the chance to take some great pictures of the wildlife and I thought it would keep me busy for the entire day.

Following the path, I strolled, looking around at every tree, flower, and bird until I finally heard the noise of the waterfall.

My senses sharpened, as my heart raced and my feet began to rush until, with the roaring of the water getting closer, I reached the first sight of the falls.

I had been to Niagara Falls, but this was something different. It would have been like comparing the Amazon River with the Yukon River. The latter is quite long, but nothing compared with the first one.

Speechlessly, open-mouthed, I took my first glance, and I snapped a couple of shots with the confidence of a man who's seen it all. When I resumed my walk, I realized what I'd first seen was only a small part of the whole complex. The more that was revealed to my eyes, the more I understood the true extent.

Unable to fully grasp what I had in front of me, I sat down for a second to process that view. I could lose my sight in search of their end, but either because of the mist or their dimensions, I couldn't find it.

A few long minutes passed by before I decided to keep strolling, intending to look forward to seeing the other side of this natural wonder, and the more I proceeded, the more I was amazed.

"And they say this is the dry season. Think about what this would look like during the wet one!" I marveled, looking at them.

I couldn't find any adjectives to describe what I saw and how it reflected in terms of sensations or thoughts. My mind got scrambled, and words failed me, wondering how I'd describe my day to my therapist. The path brought me to a small square where a statue was placed at its center.

"Dr. Livingstone, I presume..." I said aloud, glancing at the statue of the Scottish doctor and explorer, who was the first European to discover the Mosi-oa-Tunya Falls, which means "the smoke that thunders." In fact, there was a lot of smoke produced by the small particles of water, and it was genuinely thundering in a deafening sound. I looked at it and tried to figure out what that place would have looked like when he saw it.

"I can imagine your feelings, my friend." I smiled at the statue.

It's hard to say whether I was caught in up admiration of the place, but I felt as if I were alone. Alone in front of the most incredible, spectacular show nature could put together. There wasn't anything I desired more than to spend the entire day watching it and walking around.

Following the path, I reached the last spot of the falls. This was the fall's borderline during the dry season, and by no means represented the real boundary. I was almost sure there wasn't any, and the waterfalls could stretch to an indefinite point.

Glancing at the clock, it was 2:30 P.M. Finally, my belly reminded me that I didn't have any lunch yet, and I had agreed with the driver to meet me at five. The wisest thing to do was walk back, finding, perhaps, another route to enjoy the park and have something to eat at the restaurant close to the entrance.

Although the path I chose brought me away from the waterfalls, it gave me the chance to see more of the natural surroundings. The colors of the flowers, those animals I've never seen in my life, opened my heart to the vastness of the world, in which I was just a small part.

Sneaking between bushes, running behind birds, brought me back to my childhood and interrupted every time I took pictures of that marvelous, magical world.

This little child from the city who sees for the first time the nature, has never been happier. Somehow, this was the truth, as I lived in a bustling city, and the only chance of experiencing the nature was to take a walk in the park. That wasn't a real natural domain, not after I had experienced the Sahara Desert, the sub-Saharan environment, the Zambezi River, and its falls.

After that, I understood I knew nothing about what nature had to offer. It was useless to follow documentaries on TV. The feelings I had in front of these wonders were so intense, no artificial image could ever replicate them.

The image of Karen's face returned before my eyes; the power of the waters reminded me of her impetuous passion and character. She was a force of nature, and looking at the falls, I felt like she was with me.

I missed her badly, and it was almost impossible to live my life far from her. I'd have loved her to be with me to witness that natural wonder, to hold her in my arms, and have her body against mine.

"I love you, Karen. I love you more than anything in this world." Tears filled my eyes.

CHAPTER 10

Suddenly, I realized the African leg of my trip would end soon, and after it, the Asian leg would begin.

So far, I'd learned how to live in Africa, which took a lot of effort, but I knew nothing about Asia. It was like having a blank notebook in which to write a new chapter about something I ignored. Still, it was a challenge that, instead of scaring, excited me.

The only thing I hoped for was this would be more honest than the first leg of the journey. I wanted it to be free from any lies. And as I began to see improvements even without Karen, I was extremely positive as I roamed through the gates, waiting for my boarding time.

My first destination was Tbilisi, Georgia. After a long time, I'd experience the winter once again. It wasn't something I'd missed, but on the other hand, I also started to miss the chill of the air on my face.

The plane landed at Tbilisi airport at 5:15 P.M., after a flight via Istanbul. From there, it was obvious

I was no longer in Africa. Not because of the color of the skin of the people, but because of the structure itself. It matched the local cultural heritage, as it happens in every airport in the world.

The terminal appeared to be smaller than the previous ones I'd visited. For the first time, I didn't have to search for a taxi to the city center, as, since 2007, the new railway had become operational. The train station was, indeed, of modern and beautiful design and reflected the desire of the country to be competitive and attractive to tourists.

It took twenty-five minutes to reach the central station, and from there, taking a taxi wasn't an option. Although I could negotiate the price, I understood quite soon that it was more challenging to agree on a price than it was in Africa. The principal reason was that they didn't speak good English, so they kept their fare unless spoken to in Georgian.

However, even without being able to bargain for the price, I reached the hotel for a reasonable fare - or at least I hoped that was the case. After having checked the internet connection in my room, I grabbed my jacket and left the hotel. The sun was setting, and I needed to have dinner. Since the best way to get to know a country is through the food culture, I glanced around for an inspiring-looking restaurant.

In the neighborhood, there were several options for a meal, and making up my mind wasn't an easy choice. Nevertheless, since my stomach started to complain, I entered the first one on my way. I took a visual tour around and tried to figure out what kind of place it was.

Is this a place where young people come to eat, or is it more a place for families? As I was immersed in my thoughts, a young waitress arrived, smiling.

"You here for dinner?" she asked in uncertain English.

"Yes, please."

"Follow me."

I could see other people were enjoying their meals, and I had the answer to my initial question, as a heterogeneous group of customers frequented it.

At least the menu was in English, so I could read it, but I had no idea about what they would bring me. By the name, I understood only whether it was meat, fish, or a vegetarian dish. I don't have any sort of problem with food, so for the evening, I chose a meat dish with a glass of red wine.

My first taste of Georgian wine made me fall in love with it. The elegant bouquet of the sweet and spiced drink was something I couldn't quite put into words. There wasn't any memory I might have associated with it. The richness and intensity of that first sip would remain with me for the rest of my life.

I tried to fix all the details in my mind, so to give a good description of it later.

With that premise, I was looking forward to tasting my meal, and even that exceeded my expectations. I couldn't believe for such a small price, I got a fine-dining experience.

That evening, I was so excited to write about it in my diary that I forgot everything else. I needed to tell whoever was listening that, if possible, I'd quit everything and stay in that lovely city.

However, as soon as I submitted it, my telephone rang. Dr. Wright wanted to have a psychotherapy session before I went to sleep. It sounded strange, but perhaps he had his reasons for it. I'm not a psychiatrist, so I didn't want to question his procedures; he knew better. After the phone call, sudden tiredness possessed me. I went to bed, pondering what it would be like to live there with Karen.

"I need to stop thinking about her. Probably when I'm done with this therapy, she won't remember my name," I whispered as I let myself fall on the bed.

I stared at the ceiling without any steady thought in my mind. Confused and uncertain about everything, sleep didn't come to soothe my soul. But then, someone knocked on my door. I turned my glance at the clock. It was late for any sort of visit, not to mention the fact that I wasn't expecting anybody.

Gingerly, I walked to the door. "Who is it?"

Nobody answered, so I believed perhaps whoever it was had knocked at the wrong door. *That can happen.*

However, as soon as I turned around, once again, someone knocked on the door. I didn't want to open unless they identified themselves.

"Who's there?" I was almost going to lose my patience when finally, I heard someone speaking something I couldn't understand. Perhaps in Georgian.

It was a female voice. And even though I knew I shouldn't have done it, I opened the door. A tiny woman of about my same age rushed inside my room. Her long dark hair was collected into a ponytail, and her heavy makeup made me think she was going to a party. The scent of her perfume reached my senses as she came close to me.

"What?" I puzzled as she closed the door behind her.

She mentioned something, which sounded like she was in danger, but I couldn't grasp a single word.

"Do you speak any English? I don't speak Georgian," I urged.

She put a hand over my mouth. "Shh!"

Well, that was something I could understand. I watched her as she paid attention to what was going on out in the corridor. She remained like that, frozen in one moment for a while, as I tried to figure out why she'd rushed into my room. She turned to me and scrutinized me with a critical glance without saying anything. Her expression was tense, and it seemed she was wondering whether I was a bigger threat than the one she was escaping from. Then, with a deep breath, she relaxed and smiled shyly.

"Are you the American guest?"

I remained open-mouthed at her question; it was something that surprised me. "Yes. How do you know?"

"Now, I do."

"Well, how did you know there was a guest from the States?" I wondered.

"I heard someone at reception talking about an American guest, as they gave the key to your room to the cleaning staff."

"Fine, but why did you knock at my door? Are you hiding from someone?"

"Yes. Well, not exactly. I'm an escort, and the man I was accompanying questioned my price and started to raise his voice. I'm not supposed to be here, and if the staff knows it, they might call the police, and I'll be in trouble. Since he paid in advance, I tried to calm him, but he drank too much. I was afraid. Recalling your room, I decided to come here to hide. And perhaps you might have liked to spend the night with someone, rather than alone." She noticed I was in a single room.

Not convinced of what she was saying, I turned my glance at her. "Let me tell you what I think instead. There isn't any unsatisfied customer; you were trying to get me as one. However, even if you look cute, I don't sleep with prostitutes. I'm married, and happily so."

"Now, it's you who's lying." She gracefully tilted her head.

"It doesn't matter. Get out of this room before I call the reception desk."

She laughed. "I'm a better liar than you. I work at this hotel."

My jaw dropped; this woman took the words out of my mouth.

"I don't care. I didn't come to Georgia to sleep with prostitutes, and this includes you."

"Maybe you didn't, but since we are here, why miss the chance?" She leered at me, moving closer.

Considering that I already had too many problems in my life, I pushed her away. "Please, go away. I'm not going to buy any of your services." I opened the door to allow her out.

"You don't know what you are missing. But if you change your mind, this is my telephone number." She handed me a card.

Even a business card. It must be a profitable business. I shook my head as she left the room. I didn't have any idea that hotels were offering that sort of service. Although I wasn't interested, after she left, I couldn't stop thinking about her. I wouldn't have tried her services, but she made me curious, and to tell the truth, I wondered whether she told a lie or part of it. Either way, I was sure it would be difficult to fall asleep.

Perhaps the minibar in the room might help me. I opened it, and I found a couple of little bottles of whiskey. *That might be what I was looking for,* I thought, getting a glass from the bathroom.

It was late, and after a generous drink, my eyelids became heavy, and finally, I fell asleep.

However, that night, I couldn't sleep well. For the whole night, my sleep was cursed by nightmares, and when someone knocked at my door the next morning at 11:30 A.M., it was like someone drove over me with a truck. It took me what seemed like an eternity to stand on my feet, as whoever was on the other side of the door, insistently knocking, became my enemy number one.

"I'm coming. Please, a bit of patience," I panted as I got dressed.

I opened the door, and a man with two officers asked me if they could come in.

"Yes, of course. I just woke up, so it's messy." I welcomed them in.

"We're sorry for this inconvenience. I'm Detective Giorgi Bochorishvili, and those are Officers Esadze and Kazbegi," he said, introducing himself and his colleagues.

"I don't understand. Is there anything wrong?"

"You can say so. Between yesterday evening and this morning, a woman has been killed in this hotel." He took out a picture and showed it to me. "Have you ever seen her?"

I took it in my hand and scrutinized it. She looked familiar, but my mind was still foggy.

"I don't think so. I'm not sure, though. Maybe I've seen her around," I muttered, still sleepy. "Is she a guest?"

"Not really. She's an escort and used to go around telling people she works here - which isn't true - offering a safe sexual service." As he explained, the other two officers searched around.

"A murder..." I whispered to myself, trying to recall whatever happened the evening before, knowing that my brain would have messed up some, if not all, the details. However, something I was sure about was I hadn't killed anyone, nor had I heard anything coming from the corridors.

If there had been a murder, the assassin must have been very cautious in not making any noise, I considered.

"Are you sharing this room with anyone else?" asked the Detective.

"No, I'm alone."

"Could you explain this, then?" He raised a lipstick from the floor. "It doesn't seem to be your shade."

I stared at it, not knowing what I should say.

"So?" he challenged, crossing his arms across his chest.

"I don't - I don't remember."

"Let's put it this way," he started to say, "I'm not here to bring someone to jail for having sex with a prostitute, but to nail a killer. Are you telling me the truth when you say you haven't seen this woman?"

Panic possessed me. Being a liar shouldn't include necessarily becoming a murderer, and for no reason in this world would I ever kill someone. With incoherent mumbling, I explained to him what happened the previous night. I guessed it would be wiser to tell what happened. After all, I didn't have sex with her, nor did I kill her. He didn't seem impressed by my explanation. Shaking his head, he turned his eyes to the two officers.

"Your position is quite difficult, and I've got no choice but to bring you with me to the Police Department. You will be interrogated in the presence of an office lawyer. I suggest you have more solid evidence than a drunken night to get out of it."

With that, one of the policemen came to cuff me.

"Hold on! I'm not an assassin, and perhaps I've better proof than you think," I protested, refusing to be cuffed. I took my scarf and showed him the camera.

"I'm on a therapy trip." I explained the deal with Dr. Wright. "This camera is supposed to record everything I do. If something happened yesterday evening, this thing recorded it. Please, let me call my psychiatrist. He can explain everything," I added.

Detective Bochorishvili narrowed his eyelids, trying to decipher what I was saying. "You come with us to the Police Department. We'll bring your camera with you, and we'll get in touch with your doctor. If it's so, we'll ask to have the recording, and if it proves you are innocent, then we'll let you go. But as it is now, you haven't yet given any solid proof."

I was brought to a room of the Police Department, and with a hands-free phone, they asked me to dial the number of my psychiatrist.

As I expected, Dr. Wright explained the situation, confirming I was on a therapy trip, and he would forward them the content of the camera. I was left alone in the room, and thousands of thoughts came to my mind. I tried to recall what happened and whether it was me who killed the girl. Nothing definitive came up, and I was afraid I'd be condemned for a murder I didn't commit.

Time passed slowly, and I started speculating about the reason why I was left alone. Were they watching me, trying to determine my guilt from my behavior? I scanned around and noticed the mirror on my back. *How could it be I didn't see its presence as we walked into this room?*

At that point, the best thing to do was to keep calm. There wasn't any proof against me, and Dr. Wright sent them the camera recording. *Perhaps they are watching it, and soon, I'll be released,* I thought, in the attempt to convince myself.

Nevertheless, they didn't come back until a few hours later. As the door opened, I jumped in my chair, struggling to guess their verdict.

"It's true, and you are in therapy. However, the recording didn't show everything, as it was covered. Besides this detail, it did record the conversation you had with the girl, and what happened after she went away," Detective Bochorishvili concurred.

I remained silent; I was waiting for the final verdict.

"You left the room at a certain point during the night, exactly at 1:15 A.M., and you came back at 2:45 A.M. We'll take some samples of your DNA, and then we'll need to wait for the results of the autopsy. We need to know what happened last night because, by the chat we had with your psychiatrist, it was clear we can't trust your words."

They were right, but I was also sure I couldn't kill anyone. Moreover, I couldn't remember leaving the room at any time of night.

"I still can't understand how I can't recall a single detail about last night." I was in disbelief.

"The amount of alcohol you ingested was enough to give you a good hangover, and consequently, also amnesia. I can't tell if your memory will come back or not, but this is something we have to deal with," he confirmed, taking a pause.

"This morning, at 7:00 A.M., I received a call from the hotel. The receptionist told me to come quickly, as the cleaning lady found the corpse of a woman inside the storage room, where the trolley and other items are kept.

"What we saw wasn't something pleasant. My first impression was that she was killed somewhere else and dragged to that room. This was also confirmed by the marks on her shoes and on the floor. According to those marks, she was murdered in the restrooms. In this hotel, there aren't more than 30 guests. Most of them are families with children, so our suspicion narrowed to a bunch of single travelers. However, only in your room, we found her lipstick, and you admitted she came in, proposing her services. You have to admit this puts you in a difficult position."

"I understand, but I don't have any reason to kill anyone. Why would I kill a woman I've never met?

101

Regardless of whether we had sex or not, which I can't recall at all," I replied.

"This is something we hoped you could help with, but either you prefer not to tell - and in this case, you make our job more difficult - or you don't remember. One thing for sure is that one way or another, we'll reach the truth. If you are innocent, you will be free to go without any problem. If not, you will be charged with homicide and will be judged according to the Georgian laws."

They brought me back to the hotel, but they put a guard outside the door, so I couldn't leave. Technically, I was under arrest, but since they didn't have any absolute proof to nail me, they had to keep me in sight - at least until the DNA test proved me innocent, or there was some other evidence against someone else.

The wait was unbearable. The hours seemed like months, and in my head, thousands of thoughts chased each other. I wondered whether Karen knew about this terrible suspicion, or my parents, my supervisor, and Stewart. My mind raced with all the possibilities.

Will I be condemned to a life sentence? Will the U.S. Embassy be able to bring me back home? Is there anyone who can help me?

Scanning the surroundings, I thought about the possibility to use my telephone to call home or not.

I glanced at the guard, who was standing by the door.

"Can I at least call my family?" He said something in Georgian, so obviously, even if I were allowed, he wouldn't understand.

Unwilling to give up, I showed him the mobile phone and repeated the question, trying to help with gestures. He nodded but showed me I was allowed to make only one call.

I had to be wise. Who was the right person in this case? My father would do everything he could, but before he could help me, he would have a heart attack from knowing his son was detained in Georgia, suspected of murder. I decided to call Stewart, asking him to contact my family, and also Karen.

With a deep breath, I dialed his number.

That was the most intense phone call I'd ever made. In the beginning, I started to cry like an idiot, unable to describe clearly what had happened. It took me a considerable effort to be able to calm down. I gave him the telephone number of my psychiatrist, my father, and Karen. He would get in touch with Dr. Wright first, to better understand the situation and receive some advice on who to call after, and how to handle those calls.

He promised to do everything in his power and assured me I'd come home soon.

"Ethan, now, you have to keep your mind focused. Don't give up; everything will be fine. You are a liar, not a murderer," he tried to reassure me.

"Thank you, Stewart. I don't know what to think. Everything is so surreal."

The guard came to me, took my telephone, and ended the call.

CHAPTER 11

In the evening, finally, Detective Bochorishvili arrived in my hotel room.

"I've good news and bad news," he started, without saying *'hello.'* "The good news is you can stay out of prison. The bad one is we found traces of your sperm on her clothes and mouth. Therefore, you had sex with her, but you didn't necessarily kill her. The real problem is the time frame. You left the room between 1:15 A.M. and 2:45 A.M. The girl died between 2:30 A.M. and 3:00 A.M. This means you might or might not be the killer, but until we have a full reconstruction of what happened that night, I'm afraid you are the main suspect."

I gaped at him. No memories of any sexual act were left in my brain, nor did I recall leaving the room at any time during the night. "I-I don't remember having sex with her. There must be some sort of error. Are you sure that we're talking about my DNA?"

"We're 100% positive about it. I'm sure you know there's no way to share the same DNA with another person. That's the unique signature of your body. I've no idea how it's possible to have such a black hole in your memory, but Dr. Wright is coming to have a talk with you. With his help, we might come to a solution. He believes with hypnosis, we'll get some more information out of you."

A deep abyss opened under my feet, ready to swallow me for eternity. As my life as a free man started to fade away in front of my eyes, I realized I was crying.

"I was wondering if I could call my parents, or people close to me, at least once a day?" I needed to stay in touch with my life, and with those people who meant everything to me, who could assure me I wasn't a ruthless assassin.

Detective Bochorishvili took a deep breath and considered the situation for a moment. "Only once per day, and not more than five minutes to the same number. We'll give you another telephone where the numbers you want to call are stored," he said, glaring.

It wasn't enough for me to talk for such a short time a day. "What about visits? If my father comes here, will I be able to see him?"

"Like all the other prisoners, you will have the right to meet your father once a week for one hour.

You have to understand that even if you are not in jail, you are the main suspect in a murder."

"How did the girl die?" So far, they told me she got murdered, but not a word about how.

"She was strangled with the strap of her purse. According to the forensics, she had been killed in two stages. The first attempt only made her unconscious, then the killer might have understood she was still alive, so he kept strangling her until he could be sure she was dead."

I shook my head, thinking about that girl. "Will I be transferred to jail?"

"Since your case is complicated, we're going to proceed a bit differently. We'll let your psychiatrist try hypnosis to throw some light on what happened that night. If he can give us solid proof of your innocence, you will be free to go. In the opposite case, you will be considered the murderer, and you will face trial. At that point, my job is done, and you are in the hands of the judge and your lawyer," he explained briefly.

"How am I supposed to get a lawyer?"

"You know the drill. If you can't afford one, an office lawyer will be assigned to you."

"May I contact my Embassy? Perhaps they can help me somehow," I asked.

"Let's see first whether you need a lawyer or not. There's no hurry for that." He left.

I can't explain the feelings I was dealing with. Of course, this meant my therapy was suspended, and I couldn't imagine what would happen from that moment on.

The day after, I was brought to the Police Department once again, where I could finally meet Dr. Wright. His presence was comforting, and I hoped he could discharge me from all the accusations.

After a brief introduction, we were left alone. The whole session would be recorded, but I wasn't thinking about that. Without saying a word, he started the hypnosis.

When I woke up, Dr. Wright smiled at me. "You did very well. Everything will be fine," he tried to reassure me. However, despite his tone of voice, I didn't feel safe yet. My future still appeared uncertain.

Once again, I was left alone in the room, as Dr. Wright went to talk about the results with Detective Bochorishvili.

I was alone with all my thoughts and growing paranoia.

Losing track of time, I was afraid they would leave me there for the rest of my life. I already figured everybody was gone, and the locked door would never open again.

In my distorted perception of time and space, I imagined dying of starvation and dehydration because I killed a woman, about whom I couldn't recall a single detail.

In the silence of the room, I wept. "I didn't kill her; please, believe me. I'm a liar, not a killer."

My whisper raised in volume, hoping someone was still there, listening to my plea.

I've no idea about how much time passed since Dr. Wright left me alone in the room. But when the door opened, and Detective Bochorishvili came in with Dr. Wright, I didn't feel relieved.

They weren't smiling, and I was sure I was going to jail once and for all. At that point, only a good lawyer could have helped me, and the best way was either contacting my father to ask for help, or hoping for some help from the Embassy.

One thing was for sure: I didn't want to end up in prison in a foreign country for a crime I was sure I didn't commit.

"Mr. Jackson," Detective Bochorishvili exhaled. "I'm afraid we can't release you."

"What do you mean? I didn't kill her!"

"Let me finish." He grinned sternly.

Dr. Wright grabbed his arm as a warning to be more considerate. "What Detective Bochorishvili wanted to say is nothing conclusive came out of your hypnosis. The alcohol blurred many details; your mind filled up with contrasting ones that might have been made-up."

"So, I'm such a liar that even under hypnosis, I tell lies?" I lamented hopelessly.

Dr. Wright glanced at Detective Bochorishvili. "Can I have a moment to talk to my patient?"

Detective Bochorishvili simply nodded and left.

"Dr. Wright, please. I'd never do anything like that," I pleaded as soon as we were alone.

"I'm aware of that, Mr. Jackson, but I need to be honest," he admitted. "The results were inconclusive. I believe the alcohol you drank was too much for your brain to record things correctly. You should have refrained from drinking."

"This isn't helping me. I don't want to go to jail in this country. In fact, I don't want to go to jail based on suspicion. I want the truth just as much as the police do!" I started raising my voice.

"Keep calm, please. I'll try my best."

I didn't know whether he was trying to help because he cared about himself and the results of the research, or because he cared about me. In either case, I wanted to believe him. I desperately needed to trust him.

They brought me to jail to await the day of my trial.

My father came to visit me; he was in touch with one of the best lawyers he could afford, but obviously a better chance was offered by a lawyer from the Embassy. They assured me they had better knowledge of Georgian laws and could defend me better than anyone else.

It was a pity that, at that point, nothing could reach me anymore. I'd lost all hope, and I was passively waiting for the day they would confirm my final sentence.

Unaware what the penalty for that crime was, I expected to be charged with all sorts of criminal offenses, from consorting with a prostitute to murder.

During that hopeless wait, I lost any interest in life. Perhaps I also hoped I'd be given the death penalty, even without knowing whether it existed in Georgia.

What mattered to me was that I needed to wake up from that nightmare.

In the jail where I was transferred, other people were waiting for their trial, but none of them seemed to speak any English. I wasn't in the mood to talk anyway. I wanted to die.

The day after, I met a lawyer who would defend me. She was sent from the Embassy, and a slight light of hope started to shine on me when I saw her.

She was a woman in her forties, wearing a business suit and a serious expression. She somewhat reminded me of those legal crime series I used to watch on TV. I hoped that, like in those shows, even in my case, my lawyer could save the day.

"I had the time to examine your case in detail, Mr. Jackson, but I'd like to hear something directly from you." Averting her glance from me, she opened a black agenda book.

"I've got nothing to say." Bitterness poisoned the tone of my voice.

"Not even whether you are innocent or guilty?"

"Does it matter?"

"At least, for the defense I must work on." She glanced at me, biting her lower lip.

"I'm on a therapy trip. I'm supposed to get cured of compulsive lying behavior, so perhaps what I'll say is a lie..."

"I also need to know about the lies. I'm used to working with liars." A slight smile appeared on her face.

With a long exhale, knowing I had nothing to lose by telling her whatever my brain was allowing me to remember, I began. "That night, I was ready to go to sleep, but I heard someone knocking on my door," I tried to recall, hoping my mind would cooperate with me. "As I opened the door, a woman came in, saying something about an unsatisfied customer. I asked her to leave, as I was dead tired, but she insisted that, since she was there, we could have fun together. I pushed her out of the room, and since I couldn't sleep, I drank something from the minibar. The morning after, the Police came and arrested me for murder."

"Yes, I'm aware of the rest. I talked with Dr. Wright, and he gave me a clear idea of your current situation. I asked you to tell me the story because, even if you are a liar, I need your point of view," she exhaled.

"I've no idea about what happened during the hypnosis. Do you know any details?"

"For this, you should ask Dr. Wright. As his patient, you have the right to know, and he can give you a better description of it. As for me, I need to collect every single bit of information to understand the dynamic and prepare your defense for the trial."

"Do you think I have any chance to go back home? Will I be judged guilty and condemned to life imprisonment?"

She averted her gaze from me. "It's too early for me to make any prediction. If you are deemed guilty, the Embassy will work hard to make sure you will be extradited to a prison in the States."

I wasn't sure whether this was something positive or not. What I knew was I didn't want to end up in jail, not in Georgia or in the U.S.

Of course, being in a familiar environment would help psychologically, but the result was the same. I was going to lose everything: my family, job, and, most of all, any chance to get back with Karen.

CHAPTER 12

The following week, the pretrial took place, but nothing definitive came as a result that would resolve my situation.

My lawyer predicted a long battle during the trial, and the only thing I had left to do was wait.

Dr. Wright and the lawyer sent from the Embassy, Janet Wilson, transferred me from the prison to house arrest at the Hotel on the ground of my mental status and the therapy I was following.

The biggest challenge was remaining sane with the uncertainty of being condemned, perhaps, to life imprisonment. My lawyer assured me this would never happen, and I'd be extradited to the States. However, I couldn't stop worrying about the possibility of spending the rest of my life there.

The jury wasn't convinced about the psychological assessment my psychiatrist gave. They believed it was biased on his desire to have me cleared of all accusations.

I didn't have the impression Dr. Wright wanted to save me in any way. I thought, instead, he was trying to get me in trouble. His statement could be interpreted so that, although I didn't have murderous tendencies, the altered state from the alcohol eventually triggered violent behavior. According to his evaluation, I practically was the killer.

For this reason, I had to go through not just one psychological assessment, but several, of which I lost count. I was so stressed and confused that I was sure I didn't give a good impression of myself. My only hope was that they would consider my altered state of mind and interpret my answers accordingly.

The trial went on for two months until the day came when the judge was satisfied with all the evidence against me and was ready to give his verdict.

My family was supportive, and even if only my father could come for a couple of days, he kept contacting me, keeping my morale from falling into depression.

Then, there was nothing that could make me smile. I was tired of everything, even of being alive. If I couldn't be free, then I didn't want to live.

Although I didn't remember anything about what had happened, let alone about having sex with her, I knew I didn't kill the woman. It didn't much help that friends and family believed me. According to all the people who mattered in determining my fate, I was the ruthless monster who had sex with a prostitute and killed her afterward.

Nobody thought for a second that there was the possibility she died after I left her, and eventually she had been a victim of another maniac. The fact that only my sperm had been discovered had convinced everybody that I was the murderer, and what was worse, I was also starting to believe it.

I didn't hear anything from Karen, either. At that point, I was sure she didn't want to have anything to do with me. Dealing with a pathological liar is frustrating. When that liar is also accused of murder, we have that sort of situation from which everyone wants to walk away.

It was eight o'clock in the morning, and I was in my hotel room, waiting for the final trial - which was scheduled to take place the following week - when the door opened, and the guard announced a visitor.

I wasn't expecting anyone to come to see me. All my friends and family were in the States, and we could connect only by phone once a day. Generally, whoever wanted to talk to me gathered at my parents' house, and I could have a short chat with them.

I saw her come in with a confused expression in her eyes, which described the long journey to reach my hotel and all the questions she had been asking herself during this trip. Her hair was a bit ruffled, and she didn't wear any sort of make-up.

She was more beautiful than I had even recalled. Her sudden appearance in the room felt like the sun had arrived after an endless, dark winter.

Obviously, she didn't consult Dr. Wright, as he would have forbidden her to come and see me. Perhaps that would have been the best idea, but we both knew we needed to see each other to understand what we wanted from our lives.

"Hi." Her voice was tired and broken by tears that started to collect in her eyes.

Uncertainly, I got to my feet, unable to make a sound. I wanted to hug her, kiss her, tell her how my life had been meaningless until that moment. My only hope was that she didn't bother to take that long trip just to say *'goodbye.'*

"Karen, you... I was afraid you didn't want to see me anymore. I..."

She sat down in a chair and stared at me, trying to control her emotions. "Ethan, Dr. Wright called me, telling me what happened to you. There isn't a steady thought I can grab, and it has been difficult for me to decide to come to visit you. I think I know you well enough to be sure this is a misunderstanding. Nothing can convince me that you could ever kill someone."

"Not even I believe I'd be capable of anything like that. Nevertheless, there are so many holes in what

117

happened that night. According to what I remember, after she left my room, I drank a couple of whiskeys and fell asleep. The camera, instead, recorded that I left the room between 01:15 and 02:45. Also, they found traces of my sperm, so apparently we had sex, but I can't recall a single detail."

She shook her head. "Dr. Wright told me about it, too, but I think something doesn't fit. I can't stop thinking you were the wrong person at the wrong place at the right time. Who's your lawyer?"

"Her name is Janet Wilson," I replied. "She works for the Embassy, but I don't know how you can reach her. She's also of your same opinion. From her point of view, some details in the story don't fit. She has been working hard on this case, and I hope she'll find the missing piece of this puzzle."

"I need to talk to her. I can't stand to see you being accused of a crime you didn't commit. Perhaps she can give me more information about your case. I'll find her." She stood on her feet.

"Where are you going?"

"I'll be back as soon as I can. Don't you worry."

I was left alone again with my doubts, wondering what Karen might have in her mind. Whatever it was, I hoped she would succeed. My brain started to race with the possibility that, with her help, my lawyer could find a new way to discharge me from the accusations.

***

Janet Wilson, the lawyer from the Embassy, was working on the case, trying to grasp a detail that could make sense in that intricate story. She didn't believe Ethan was a killer. In her whole career, she had seen many people - liars, murderers, thieves, and innocents - and that was an innocent man.

"But how to prove that?" she wondered.

She took all the documentation she received from the Police Department: the report from the Forensics and the photographs shot in the bathroom and in the storage room. There, she had the pictures of the shoe impression taken after spraying luminol, which detected traces of blood and sperm that could be isolated from the other organic residue. One thing that attracted her attention was the photo they took when recovering the shoe impression.

"Something is missing here." She took a careful look at the picture. "Damn! I need the original image. These don't tell me the whole truth."

She grabbed the phone and called the Forensics Office. She wanted to speak with the same person who took the pictures and analyzed the footprints. He promised to send her the original digital images that were taken.

As she was waiting for them to arrive at her email address, a woman was brought into her office by one of her colleagues.

119

"Janet, this is Ms. Karen Kühn. She's Mr. Jackson's girlfriend." She came inside the room, followed by a guest.

Janet raised her gaze from the pictures and scrutinized Karen. "Oh," she said. "Please, take a seat."

"Thank you. I just came from the hotel where Ethan is being detained," Karen started to explain. "He told me what he knows about the murder, and to me, it doesn't make sense. I've no idea whether you are aware of this or not, but my boyfriend is a pathological liar. He's on a therapy trip, so I came here to get a better idea of what is going on. I'm not informed of all the details, but I know him, and he isn't a killer. He's a liar, but this isn't a crime, is it?"

"No, it isn't, and to be honest, I'm trying my best to figure out what has happened. I need to reconstruct this complex puzzle piece by piece."

There was a short pause of silence, where Karen tried to guess Janet's thoughts.

Then, Janet jumped up. "Come with me. We're going to take a tour of the hotel. I might need some help."

They spent the whole afternoon at the hotel, examining every detail of the premises: the position of the camera, the recordings, the timing - every single detail.

"I think I need to get back to my office and brainstorm alone. I hope the material I've asked from the Forensics has arrived, and if we're lucky, we might put an end to this unfortunate case." Janet took a deep breath.

"Please, keep me updated about any progress. I'm so worried." Karen crossed her fingers, bringing her hands to her chest.

***

It was only after three days, in the late evening, that Detective Bochorishvili came inside my room, accompanied by my lawyer.

Detective Bochorishvili had a strange expression on his face. It seemed like shame, anger, and relief all mixed together. He tried his best to avoid looking into my eyes.

"I've got great news," my lawyer said happily.

"What kind of news?" I stood from my chair.

"You are free to go," Detective Bochorishvili almost whispered.

I stared at them, not quite sure whether I understood it correctly or not.

"But... how?" Unable to understand how it was possible that the previous day I was considered the most wanted assassin in Georgia, and then I was free to go, I gaped.

"I've been examining the whole case at least a thousand times, and as I mentioned to you, there was something unclear. Days ago, when your girlfriend appeared in my office, she made me think about one detail I left aside. Suddenly, I got it; it was the time frame that was completely wrong," she explained. "Once again, I called the forensic pathologists, and I requested all the details to be sent to my email address, including the digital pictures in the original format. I asked to have every bit of information possible. I also needed to know the location of surveillance cameras in this hotel, so I returned here to find out that those are installed in the elevators and at the entrance.

"At that point, I was sure I had all the pieces of the puzzle. What I had to do was to put them together and try to get something that made any sense."

I began to try to unravel the end of the story, but since I had no memories of what happened that night, I believed this was my best chance to get a reconstruction of the facts.

She took a deep breath and continued speaking. "From the cameras placed at the entrance, we ascertained she came back to the hotel at 1:43 A.M.

"Supposedly, you were waiting for her in the lobby and walked together to the restroom, where you decided to take advantage of her offer.

"From the forensics, I retrieved the following information: first, you had oral sex with her, and this means you couldn't have killed her during the act. It also tells us that, considering the amount of alcohol you ingested, it would have taken something like forty minutes for you to reach orgasm or any sort of satisfaction. This detail reveals that you were ready to go back to your room at 2:28 A.M.

"Of course, we need to consider the time you would have needed to kill her, counting on her struggle to escape from you. Afterward, you would have had to hide her body, which was found in a storage room close by. To do so, you would have had to ensure nobody could have seen you dragging her there from the restrooms.

"To arrive at your room, considering that the cameras in the elevators confirmed you used it only to reach the first floor from your room, you had to walk for eleven minutes. In this case, you should have been back to your room later than the time recorded by your camera.

"So, someone else was in the restrooms, waiting for me to leave to kill her?" I almost couldn't believe it.

"Indeed, but we found more proof that it wasn't you who killed the girl," she commenced. "I spent the whole night looking at those pictures. Something that wasn't considered was that there must have been two people in the restrooms. You, who had sex with the victim. The other was hiding in one of the toilets, waiting for you to leave. This became obvious when I was observing the shoe impressions. From them, it seemed you walked away, and perhaps she was standing up from her kneeling position when someone assaulted her. We can't tell the time frame, but obviously, it wasn't your footprint that dragged her body to the storage room, where she was found the morning after."

"That is a feasible conclusion," growled Detective Bochorishvili. "We'll look further to find him."

My lawyer smiled at us. "We've just come from the Courthouse, where the judge, in light of the new evidence, decided to drop all the charges against you."

I heard what she said, and yet, I couldn't understand a single word. "Really? I mean, are you saying I'm free to go?"

"Well." Detective Bochorishvili stretched his shoulders. "Not really. You still had sex with a prostitute, and under Georgian law, that's illegal."

"However..." Impatiently, Mrs. Wilson cut him off. "You will be charged with a fine, which will be decided tomorrow during a private session with the judge."

Open-mouthed, I was left speechless. Evidently, I was going to be in trouble for having paid for sexual services, but this was better than being accused of murder. Hopefully, I could fly away from here, and I might also resume my therapy.

The only thing I wanted was to be back home, far from all sorts of unwanted adventures. For once, I was missing my old, boring life so badly. I just wanted to be home with Moses.

Though, I knew nothing could be like it was before I started this trip. Still, I had to figure out my life, and now, there was a new element to be added: Karen. I didn't want to live my life without her, but we needed to understand what we were expecting from our relationship.

The only thing I was sure about was I loved her, and I'd do everything to make our relationship work. Besides, my therapy showed remarkable progress when I was with her, and I couldn't care less if it was because of her, or because of the treatment itself.

With her, I didn't lie anymore, and it was all I needed. I hoped it was also enough for her. I wanted to use the rest of my vacation to try and build a life with Karen. What was important was I was no longer a liar.

Nevertheless, before being able to think about moving to Germany, I had to first return to the States. There were several reasons for this decision; one of them was Moses. I needed to have my friend with me, then I needed to take some final tests after the funded therapy.

We decided I'd spend six months in Germany, and afterward, she would move to the States for another six months. I didn't know what would come after; presumably, we'd figure it out day-by-day.

The sensation of the plane leaving the Georgian ground was indescribable. I was sure my life was going to end in jail in Tbilisi, far from my family and all the people dear to my heart. Most of all, I was afraid I'd lost Karen forever. She was the only hope I had for a healthy life, free from my lying behavior.

I wanted to laugh and cry, all at once. Looking around myself at the other people on the plane, it was so surreal. Leaning down in my seat, sinking into the soft, comfortable, first-class seat offered by the Embassy, all the positive memories I had from that trip returned to my mind.

Behind my closed eyes, I could once again see the almost interminable extents of the African Savanna. The mighty roars of the lions came distinctly to my ears. In my mind I also recalled the silence of the Sahara Desert, and I remembered my first impression of it: the biggest sandbox in the world.

A chuckle came out of my mouth as I thought about Moses...

At that point, I started to cry.

Never in my life had I felt so threatened and relieved at the same time. The simplest of thoughts were the most treasured I had.

We care about the wrong things, I thought. Then, slowly, exhaustion won over my emotions, and I fell asleep.

The bump of the plane landing in London woke me up. I didn't know what time it was; the only thing I knew was I was hungry.

There were a couple of hours until the departure of the connecting flight, so without thinking twice, I sat down at the first restaurant I could spot.

As I was looking at the menu, I realized one crucial thing: something was different, like an incomplete puzzle, or a drawing that has been ripped just where the most beautiful part was.

In the beginning, I couldn't focus on what was wrong until I saw myself reflected in a mirror.

I appeared older, more tired...

I was different, not the world or anything else.

With a slow movement, I raised a hand to touch my face, to be sure it was really me who was reflected in the mirror.

All my doubts were slowly fading away, like the shadows of a nightmare at dawn, and I was the man who began to understand his place in the Universe.

Thinking about all the events that shaped my last months, it sounded like a joke - a bad one, too. Nevertheless, that joke was my life, and I was determined to live it, enjoy it, and to give it meaning.

I don't remember what I ordered. It was probably the first thing that came to my eyes, and when the server brought it to me, it tasted like heaven.

The landing of the plane at the Boston Logan airport marked the end of that adventure, and a surreal feeling grabbed me as I waited to collect all the luggage in the baggage claim.

My father and my mother were the first people I could see. Stewart was also there. A moment of hesitation, when I tried to decide whether I was dreaming or not, and with tears in my eyes, I ran to hug them.

The nightmare was over, and I was free. Although I was still a liar, I wasn't a murderer.

It took several days before I went back to meet Dr. Wright and Prof. Doyle. I needed to go on with my life, and I was also scared of their reaction to what happened in Tbilisi. I was afraid they would blame me for the failure of the therapy, and consequently, the research.

Nevertheless, regardless of everything that had happened, they had been kind to me. Their only regret was not being able to go through with the whole project.

"You don't have to be sorry. There's nothing you could have done differently that would have changed the result. Too many players had their role in the failure of this project. Some of them could have been avoided if we were more careful," Dr. Wright objected.

"Indeed, it was bad luck. Hopefully, you will benefit from this part of the therapy," Prof. Doyle added.

"I'm thankful for the chance given. I hope I'll be more honest from now on. Perhaps I'll get back to you for an additional psychotherapy session." I shrugged, almost joking.

"You know where to find me. So, what are your plans, if I'm not too indiscreet?" Dr. Wright asked.

"I'll move to Germany with Karen for the next six months. We'll use that time to understand whether our relationship has a future or not. The way I see it is that with her, my brain worked more honestly."

"I think it's a good plan, but remember, at this point, you don't have any means to tell whether your illness has been improved or not," cautioned Dr. Wright. "I'd like you to come to visit me one last time before your departure to assess your condition."

"I'll make an appointment with your secretary as soon as I reach home. Thank you very much, once again, for the opportunity."

I left the room, confident that in the end, there would be a solution for everything. My life would finally know some sort of normality.

EPILOGUE

-In Prof. Doyle's office when he was alone with Dr. Wright-

"For one moment, I feared you were going to tell him everything about the real reason for his therapy." Prof. Doyle glanced at Dr. Wright as soon as they were alone.

"Of course, not." Dr. Wright shook his head. "Telling him we used his illness to test a new drug able to transform a common person, even the most mild-natured one, into a cold-blooded killing machine, would have been detrimental to his mental health. My aim is to help people with their issues, not to create more."

"Maybe you're right. After all, it could have put us in a difficult situation if he decided to go to the police."

"Who would have ever believed him? He's a pathological liar, and I have all the proof. He doesn't have any proof about who murdered the girl in the hotel, nor about the testing of the new drug," Dr. Wright smirked.

"Something you haven't told me is whether it was he who killed her."

Dr. Wright took a deep breath. "We might say we did it together. He did a good job, but he forgot to check that she was dead. When he saw her unconscious, he believed his work was done. I'll have to adjust the post-hypnotic order, considering we're not dealing with professional killers.

"A small detail like checking that the victim is dead might not be something obvious. In practice, as he left the restrooms, I had to continue his job. We couldn't afford to risk her going to the police."

He took a short pause. "Everything was planned, from the recruiting of the escort who came into his room, to the post-hypnotic order to get the drink from the minibar - where I added the drug we needed to test - to the murder. Modifying the recording of the camera was perhaps the most challenging part, and that's something else we must implement.

"Also changing the bottles in the minibar in his room wasn't something easy. I hope I won't have to do these kinds of tricks anymore."

"So, we can say the experiment was perfectly successful," concluded Prof. Doyle.

Dr. Wright chuckled. "Yes. We can, indeed, temporarily transform a mild-natured person who would never harm anybody into a ruthless, cold-blooded assassin who wouldn't remember anything about what happened. Our client will be satisfied with the outcome. So far, we have ten positive cases out of twelve. Even if we might consider it a good result, we need more evidence."

"This means to add more victims," replied Prof. Doyle, concerned.

"Research needs its test subjects. Whether they are rats or humans, the goal remains the same: consistent results for successful research.

"Besides, I have a great patient in my hands. She suffers from insomnia. With the right hypnotherapy and the use of our special drug, we'll transform her into a perfect killing machine for one night. The best part of all is she won't remember anything."

"Then, let's get to work. I'll prepare all the tests to make the final assessment. I hope that, like in the previous case, she'll give a positive result."

Dr. Wright grinned. "I'm almost certain of it. You will see."

I hope you enjoyed this short prelude to the series, and the way Ethan was saved at the last minute from life imprisonment in Georgia. Yet, the killers are still on the loose and they have ambitious plans for other patients and other victims. Will

Detective Bochorishvili crack the mystery? Will the Boston Police Department become interested in the case and cooperate with Tbilisi Police Department? Find out more about this case and add some pieces to this intricate, deadly puzzle in:

BACKGROUND RESEARCH

This novella is a work of fiction. However, it describes a psychological condition, which might raise some questions among the readers. The pathological lying disorder, of which my main character seems to have been affected since a young age, is considered a mental issue rather than a bad habit. Even though lying is common, it's not clear why some individuals become pathological liars.

Although pathological lying was defined in the scientific literature over 100 years ago, it has remained poorly researched. Its significance to the practice of psychiatry is mostly unclear. Pathological lying as a symptom may occur in Factitious Disorder and Borderline Personality Disorder. However, it's plausible to appear on its own and occur independently of a known psychiatric disorder.

Healy and Healy (*Healy W, Healy MT: Pathological Lying, Accusation, and Swindling. Boston: Little, Brown, 1926*) suggested that a clear distinction should be made between those who lie pathologically as a direct complication of a psychiatric disorder (secondary pathological liars, according to *Dike, Charles & Baranoski, Madelon & Griffith, Ezra. (2005). Pathological lying revisited. The journal of the American Academy of Psychiatry and the Law. 33. 342-9*), and pathological liars who do not demonstrate symptoms of a clearly defined psychiatric disorder (primary pathological liars). In fact, Healy and Healy argued that real pathological lying should be independent of a primary psychiatric disorder. In conclusion, according to Charles C. Dike, (MD, MPH, Member of the Royal College of Psychiatrists) *"Pathological lying is a special form of lying, narrow in its definition and complicated in its presentation. Its apparent rarity may be the consequence of a lack of awareness of the phenomenon by clinicians. Unfortunately, it periodically causes significant hardship to the pathological liar. Psychiatrists confronted with pathological liars should complete a thorough clinical evaluation and obtain a longitudinal history of their lies, especially through collateral information from relatives, friends, and employers. In addition to psychotherapeutic treatment, psychiatrists should consider research into the usefulness of pharmacotherapy for impulsivity or compulsive behaviors in these patients."*

Far from wanting to write research on modern and historical psychiatry, I have given more importance to details like the real plan of Dr. Wright and his team disguised into a treatment for mild psychological conditions. The explanation of the disease has been given in the story as a marginal reference.

Stay tuned by following me on:

Facebook:

Twitter:

Website:

If you want to know more about me, get informed ahead about promotions and join my ARC team, join my Newsletter. I promise I won't spam your mailbox and will send email only once a month or whenever there is important news to share:

ABOUT THE AUTHOR

Paula J. Mann lives a double life. She is a geologist by day and a novelist by night. She's best known for writing psychological thrillers and dramas, like her debut novel 'A Tale of a Rough Diamond.'

She also writes historical fiction, like Aquila et Noctua, and paranormal suspense like 'Thou Shalt Never Tell.'

Traveling is another passion, and she shares her experiences on her blog together with whatever topic raises her attention:

BIBLIOGRAPHY
Books in Italian:

Le Indagini del Commissario Scala –
Serie Completa

Inganno Fatale
– Trilogia completa

Mercante di Perle

Books in English:

Thrillers:

A Commissario Scala Mystery in
Rome – Full series

Deadly Deception – Full trilogy

Merchant of Pearls

The Ghosts of Morgan Street

A Tale of a Rough Diamond

Historical fiction:

Aquila et Noctua

Paranormal suspense:

Thou Shalt Never Tell

Made in the USA
Las Vegas, NV
21 March 2025